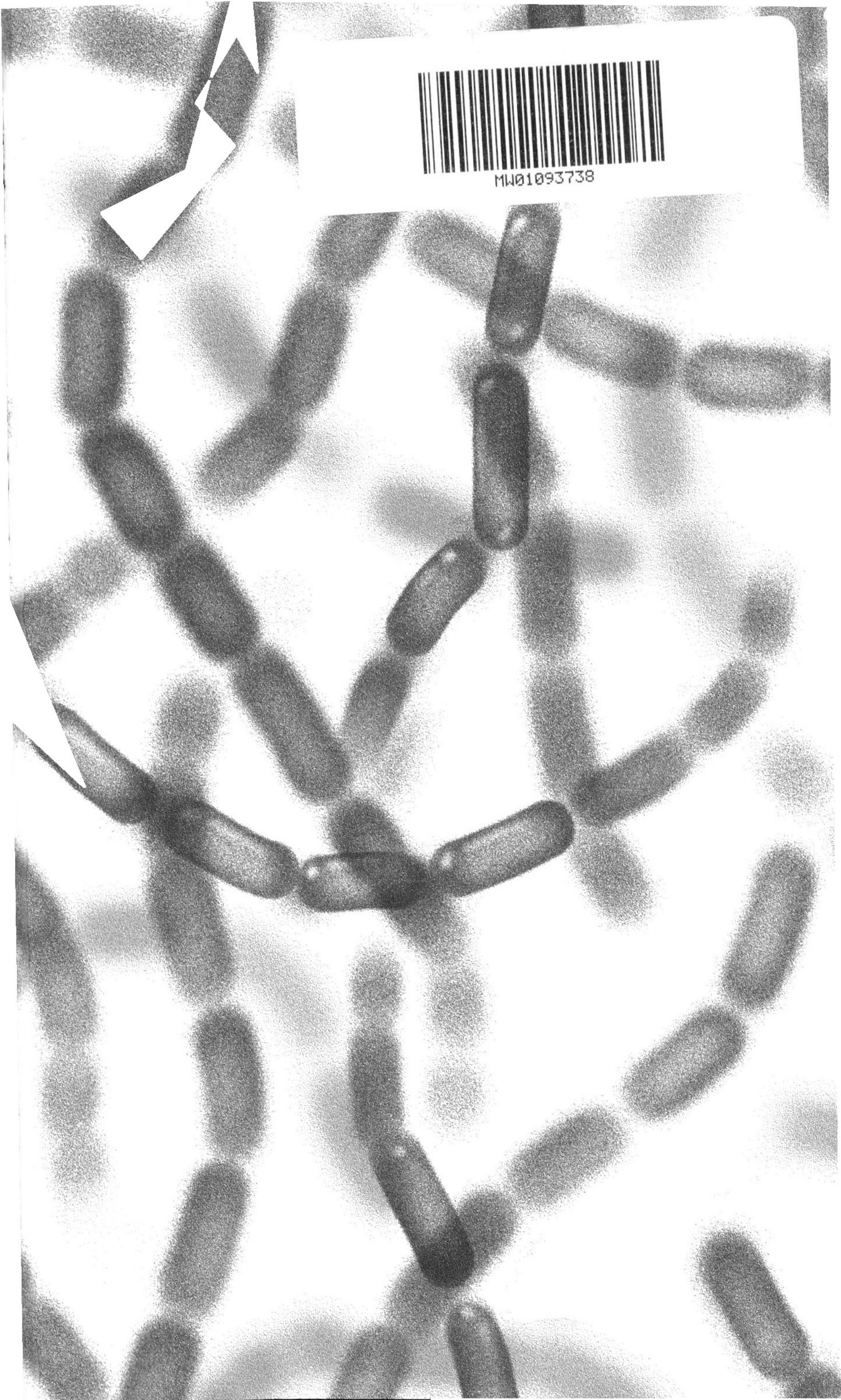
MW01093738

# HORSEFLY

**MIREILLE GAGNÉ**

translated by
**PABLO STRAUSS**

Coach House Books, Toronto

Originally published in French by La Peuplade as *Frappabord* by Mireille Gagné


First English-language edition

Canadä

Published with the generous assistance of the Canada Council for the Arts and the Ontario Arts Council. Coach House Books also acknowledges the support of the Government of Canada through the Canada Book Fund.

LIBRARY AND ARCHIVES CANADA CATALOGUING IN PUBLICATION

Title: Horsefly / Mireille Gagné ; translated by Pablo Strauss.
Other titles: Frappabord. English
Names: Gagné, Mireille, author | Strauss, Pablo, translator.
Description: First edition. | Translation of: Frappabord.
Identifiers: Canadiana (print) 20250114836 | Canadiana (ebook) 20250116758 | ISBN 9781552454992 (softcover) | ISBN 9781770568594 (PDF) | ISBN 9781770568471 (EPUB)
Subjects: LCGFT: Novels.
Classification: LCC PS8613.A436 F7313 2025 | DDC C843/.6—dc23

*Horsefly* is available as an ebook: ISBN 978 1 77056 847 1 (EPUB), 978 1 77056 859 4 (PDF)

Purchase of the print version of this book entitles you to a free digital copy. To claim your ebook of this title, please email sales@chbooks.com with proof of purchase. (Coach House Books reserves the right to terminate the free digital download offer at any time.)

*Horse fly, any member of the insect family Tabanidae (order Diptera), but more specifically any member of the genus* Tabanus. *These stout flies, as small as a housefly or as large as a bumble bee, are sometimes known as greenheaded monsters; their metallic or iridescent eyes meet dorsally in the male and are separate in the female … Adult horse flies are fast, strong fliers that are usually found around streams, marshes, and wooded areas. They may be carriers of various animal diseases such as anthrax, tularemia, and trypanosomiasis. Females deposit long, flat, black eggs in clusters; the eggs are laid on the grass. Horse flies overwinter in the larval stage, pupate in spring, and emerge as adults by late June.*

– Encyclopedia Britannica

*He sent swarms of flies among them, which devoured them.*

– Psalms 78:45

## PREDATOR

I spy you from afar, drawn by your slightest movement and, especially, the heat and carbon dioxide you exude. With great care I approach you and breathe in your scent. Each of you has a distinct smell. I must admit that I prefer your males for their tangy, earthy, unfailingly intoxicating musk. Discreetly I draw near, then nearer still. For minutes on end I flutter and flit around you in concentric circles, each one smaller than the last. I'm in luck when you are asleep and I can freely study your behaviour and breathing, the movements of your eyes beneath their lids, the pulsing of your blood in the prominent veins on your wrists and your necks. Few realize that as I circle I am hard at work, surveying those regions of your skin that, even if you felt my presence, you could never reach.

I especially love the sweltering summer nights when you lie naked in your bed with the windows open just a crack, nights when the ambient noise drowns out the buzzing of my wings. I goad and prod until you turn onto your stomach, affording access to the moist, translucent skin behind your knees. The mere thought of it makes me quiver with pleasure. Often my craving for tender flesh cannot be put off another instant. After choosing the exact place of greatest safety, I succumb: just grazing you at first but then alighting on you with these shock-absorbing legs. Such ecstasy in this initial touch, before the painful bite that lets you know, in no uncertain terms, that I am here.

Delicately I place my mouth on your smooth skin, like a warm tongue, initiating suction just strong enough to get a taste. An ineffable urge comes over me then. My head. My eyes, each moving independent of the other. My panoramic vision. My triangular wings. My hairy legs and thorax. My striped abdomen. I open my jaw slightly and pierce your outer layer of skin with my knifelike mandible. Bodily fluids ooze from the freshly opened wound. Gleefully I suck and swallow your blood, my glorious prey. Warm. Sweet. Precious. Life-giving. Sometimes I even manage to tear off a whole chunk of your flesh, which will keep me in hours of restful digestion. I do not see myself as cruel; no, I am hematophagous. Only feeding on large mammals gives me the blood meal I need to procreate. In swarms, we can extract up to a litre from our victims in a day. And yes, sometimes my bite transmits disease.

# GODDAMN HORSEFLIES

Theodore is yanked from sleep by something like a gunshot in his ear. A sharp pain shoots through his right leg. Instinctively, he slaps the back of his knee and feels something juicy and viscous between his fingers. A scowl of pain redraws his face. He vigorously rubs his skin.

'Goddamn horseflies.'

He struggles to sit up in bed, his head still spinning from the night before. A mostly finished case of beer and a scattering of empties lie behind him. It's going to be a tough day working in this heat wave, all the worse since he reluctantly agreed to do a double shift. He stands up, taking pains to stretch each joint. In recent years he's had to be more careful: his nerves are hardening like steel.

Save for the buzzing of insects, it's shockingly quiet in Theodore's apartment. No yelling or fighting from his upstairs neighbours. No sound from their TV that is never turned off. No street noise, though he lives on a busy road. Even the bedroom curtains hang perfectly still, without a breeze to make them swell from time to time. Theodore opens them and looks out the window. The city has slowed to a crawl. What's everyone doing? Where have they all hidden away? It feels as though an immense crater is about to open up beneath his feet and swallow him whole. He senses danger, but not its source or nature. A creepy feeling. Silence makes Theodore uncomfortable. As far back as he can remember, he has always hated the absence of noise, an emptiness that amplifies his own. He anxiously checks the time. It's already 1:45. He'll have to pick up the pace if he doesn't want to be late for work; his shift at the factory starts at 3 p.m. To liven up the apartment, he turns on his grandfather's old radio and takes two ibuprofen.

> A new episode of domestic violence was reported in Berthier-sur-Mer last night when a man locked himself in his home with his wife and their two children and threatened to kill them. It's the sixth case of its kind this week...

As he distractedly listens to the news, Theodore makes his way to the kitchen for a glass of Coke and a grilled cheese. His entrance disturbs three horseflies, who dart off. How did they get in? One lands on his hand. He shakes away the insect and tries to track it with his eyes. A second fly lands on him, next to his mouth. He shoos this one as well, disdainfully this time. The flies disgust him. He can never tell how they got in or what they might be carrying. Above all, he hates the sight of them rubbing their legs together; he imagines they are hatching schemes against him. Disturbed by their presence in his kitchen, Theodore forgets what he came for and grabs the swatter he keeps on top of the fridge. He goes from room to room, inspecting the apartment. Nothing's wrong with the windows in the living room or bathroom. But in the bedroom he finds a small slit in the screen. It looks like it was gnawed by some small creature. He leans in to look more closely at the breach, but just as he's about to push his index finger through, he feels a second painful bite, behind his right ear this time. Impulsively he slaps his own head. The horsefly is killed instantly, leaving a smear of red blood on Theodore's hand. He wonders if it is his own.

> … a psychologist who specializes in domestic violence. Welcome to the show. My first question: Do you believe this spike in violence we're seeing could be linked to the heat wave?

The burning pain this time is even worse than the last bite. The fly must have taken off a goodly chunk of flesh.

'Son of a bitch!'

Determined to soothe the pain, Theodore heads to the bathroom for a washcloth. How many times had his grandfather applied cold compresses when Theodore was a child? While he lets the water run until it comes out cold enough, he looks in the mirror. Sticks out his tongue. Raises his eyelids as far as they'll go, tries to smile. It's a rude awakening. He appears tired and worn. People must see him as older than he is. And dirty too: he can never quite scrub off the bluish pigment that stains his hands and forearms. With his pale skin and blond hair, he looks a little like a walking corpse. Theodore shrugs his shoulders and leaves his reflection behind. He places his hand under the water, which is running cold at last, and wets the cloth. He turns his head and folds his ear to look behind it in the mirror. A drop of blood runs the length of his neck, and another bead has coagulated on the bite. He wipes it away and firmly presses the compress to it; the burning stops. He wrings out the cloth and applies it to the back of his leg. Theodore closes his eyes, soothed, but the pain hits back hard the moment the cold subsides. He abandons the now-lukewarm cloth on the edge of the sink, and the discussion on the radio. The psychologist is still talking.

... domestic violence. For example, the extreme heat of the last few days, along with the proliferation of insects and the shutdown of a popular social media platform, can be an irritant and a trigger for sensitive individuals ... You cannot underestimate ...

By the time Theodore has showered, eaten, and dressed, it's 2:45. After putting on his work clothes and steel-toed boots, he grabs the keys to his old car and shuts the door behind him. There's no time to make a lunch. In any event, he prefers the vending machine: ham sandwich on white and an Orange Crush. For a second he regrets not duct-taping the tear in the screen before leaving, but he doesn't go back. He turns the key twice to lock the door and misses the phone ringing, his landline on the kitchen counter, drowned out by the radio droning out the day's bad news. The old answering machine clicks on and starts recording.

ham and cheese on a roll ... and an orange drink (if you know you know)

You should pay your grandfather a visit. He's been very upset. If you don't come visit, we'll have to restrain him, and you know he doesn't like that.

# THE FORBIDDEN ISLAND

*July 14, 1942*

Six fifteen a.m. Thomas glanced nervously at his watch. He was early. After setting down his suitcase at the bottom of the front steps of the Université de Montréal building on Rue Saint-Denis, he sat. A hot flash swept over him. This was the exact meeting place indicated in the telegram he'd received a few weeks earlier. Not long after his official mobilization order, Thomas had been requisitioned to serve his country in a laboratory, as an entomologist. He knew nothing further, except that it was expressly forbidden to share this information with anyone whatsoever, including his family. The brief message did not say where he was going or how long he would be there.

The days leading up to the rendezvous had felt interminable, his mind a battleground of conflicting emotions. While he was somewhat frustrated at being forced to put his own research on hold, his impatience had also been growing ever harder to contain. With a specialization like his, he had never imagined that he would be needed for the war effort.

His family said their terse goodbyes: Thomas had never been what could be called a warm person. He told them he'd been assigned important duties overseas. His father didn't seem to suspect a thing; his mother wiped away a tear. In this family, forbearance had always been the greatest kindness. Thomas had packed his suitcase, content with a bare minimum: clothing, razor, toothbrush, a family photo, and most importantly a reference book on insects.

Seven a.m. on the dot. A black car pulled up in front of Thomas. Unconsciously he held the air in his lungs for the time it took two non-commissioned Canadian army officers to step out. Both were slightly younger than him, no more than twenty-five. They promptly touched the visors of their caps in salute. Perhaps owing to their crisply ironed uniforms, Thomas didn't dare ask questions. His gut told him no answer would be forthcoming. After checking his ID papers, the NCOs took his suitcase and waved him into the car. Relieved to be absolved of the need to make conversation, Thomas obeyed in silence.

The car set off as quickly as it had arrived, driving Thomas the two miles to Windsor Station, where a train stood ready to leave. The platform was thronged with civilians and the odd soldier. Excited conversation echoed out, children ran around, one woman with a uniformed man was struggling to choke back her sorrow. Thomas could not tear his eyes away; her dress called up a vague childhood memory he couldn't quite bring into focus. She felt his eyes on her and looked at him. Then a strange expression came over her face, and Thomas looked away. He was wearing a grey suit and sweating profusely. The two NCOs ordered him to follow them into the first train car and sat down on either side of him. Thomas took his seat and tried to blend in. He wiped his forehead with his handkerchief, and before putting it back in his pocket he ran his fingers over the monogram embroidered by his mother. Certain passengers stared at him distrustfully, perhaps taking him for an enemy or a German spy. With every passing day, the tension in the air from the war was more palpable, even on this side of the Atlantic. Thomas shifted his gaze to the window and sunk down in his seat, hoping to be forgotten.

Seven thirty-two. The departure whistle blew and the train trundled off slowly to the east.

Hours passed. The monotonous landscapes of farmers' fields and grasslands and forest as far as the eye could see plunged Thomas into a near-hypnotic state. At each stop, a clamour of activity around the arriving train jerked him from his reveries. New and departing passengers stole furtive glances at him. Each time, Thomas looked at the NCOs. Finding their faces blank, he slipped back into contemplation. A little over an hour outside Quebec City, the train again drew to a halt in a small country town. The soldiers stiffened in their seats, and so did Thomas. They signalled him to get up and escorted him to the door. Outside the station there was no one but a few farmers working a load of grain. The army vehicle parked across from the station looked out of place. Thomas climbed into the back, once again flanked by the two officers, and placed his small suitcase on his knees. The sun was strong, his face undoubtedly as red as he imagined.

The truck began to move, leaving a cloud of dust in its wake. At first the driver followed the town's main street, and then he took another, quieter road along the river. They went on like this for a good twenty minutes before pulling up to a military base. Thomas knew the army had built camps along the St. Lawrence; the seaway was strategically important. But he never would have imagined this. *Why here,* he wondered. The camp was still under construction: just three buildings and a half-completed training centre. The vehicle stopped at a guard hut. A senior officer immediately stepped out, looking annoyed. He signalled that everyone should get out of the truck. After quickly shaking Thomas's hand without looking him in the eye, he ordered the soldiers to take him to the dock at Pointe-aux-Oies immediately. The other researchers had been there for some time; the tide wouldn't wait.

Thomas was led to the bay, where long platforms of rough-hewn wood planks had been laid on the banks as a makeshift dock. A steamboat was moored at the end. Gathered on the tidal flats were fifteen or so scientists. They looked like they'd been waiting for hours. The irritation on their faces betrayed the great fatigue they were attempting, surely out of pride, to conceal. Some were sitting, others stood. A few exchanged whispers when the soldiers' backs were turned. A wave of unease swept through the group. Thomas walked over and joined them, waiting for the soldiers to finish loading up.

'All aboard, *à bord!*' the captain called, at last.

None dared be first to walk the platform. Thomas stood with his feet in the sand alongside the other scientists, exchanging looks of concern. No one wanted to move forward. Thomas observed the scene: Could it really be that he was part of this? One of the officers who had escorted Thomas gave him a little shove on the back, forcing him to advance. *Like cattle to the slaughter,* he thought. All he could do was move forward. A wet-clay smell hung thick in the air. Between the slats of the makeshift dock, he could not see his reflection in the brackish water. He looked up and scanned the horizon. The other scientists were all following close behind. They crowded onto the boat every which way. Thomas stood: he knew that if he sat he'd never find the strength to get up again. Other scientists leaned up against the guardrails or sat right on the deck.

14:08. Soldiers untied the mooring lines. Thomas had the distinct feeling that there was no turning back now. The boat steamed away from the shoreline, taking him and the others to parts still unknown. The placid waters parted for them without a fight. The sun beat down on passengers and crew. Everyone struggled to find a breath of air. Luckily, the trip was just over an hour. Thomas saw a thin brown line on the horizon, followed by several smaller ones. Then, large colourless buildings rose up from the ground, like grey ghosts clinging to the rock faces. An unpleasant jolt of electricity shot down Thomas's spine. As the boat neared the shore, dozens of soldiers in khaki emerged from nearby warehouses to help with the landing, like a colony of ants preparing to meet an attack. The soldiers made busy tying lines and lowering gangways. The captain cut the motor. The officer signalled to disembark onto dry land. This time, every man obeyed. Thomas was among the first to set foot on the unfamiliar shore and tried his best to hide his unease. What awaited them on this forbidden island?

The scientists were herded together by the soldiers and lined up in front of a large hangar near the dock. Fifteen or so others, who must have arrived in the previous days, were already assembled. They looked better-rested than the new arrivals. A lieutenant called roll, scrupulously ticking off each name after noting their place of origin. Thomas counted thirty scientists: twelve from the United States, fourteen from England, and four from Canada. He hoped he'd get a chance to talk with them in coming days. For now there was no way; the soldiers were swarming around everywhere, their eyes never leaving their charges.

The researchers waited in complete silence. No one dared speak. Only the hum of nearby insects filled the emptiness, and not even a hint of breeze rose up to disperse them. One man kept swatting with his bare hands to shoo away an especially insistent fly. Thomas was still dizzy from the rolling of the boat. He had to squint against the harsh sun. Rays of light refracted off the grey rocks and exploded onto his retina. Thomas suddenly felt ill. A black curtain closed in on his field of vision and he had to crouch down to keep from fainting. One of the British scientists leaned over him, and their eyes met. Clearly, Thomas was not alone in his misgivings. After taking a deep breath, he slowly found his footing. The ground had stopped shifting beneath his feet.

16:35. A stalky man with a puffy face came out of the main hangar door, flanked by ten or so men. The abundant insignia on his uniform commanded silence all around. He introduced himself as Major Walker, chief scientist and head of operations. The Major's presence instilled unease. He rather curtly welcomed them to the War Disease Control Station and thanked them for their contribution to the mission. Thomas was surprised that this island was their final destination. When he had learned that he would be requisitioned to conduct military research, he had pictured some desert bunker in the United States or a secret laboratory in the British Isles – anywhere but this island in the St. Lawrence River. How far were they, really, from the coast and its residents? Seven or eight kilometres at most. Whatever had led them to set up a laboratory here?

Major Walker stopped speaking, and Thomas snapped back to reality. A lieutenant was handing out paperwork, in English only, for the scientists to sign. His heart clenched as he read the research confidentiality clauses. He immediately thought of his mother. He wouldn't be able to write her without lying.

*Forbidden to leave the island prior to the end of the mission.*

*Forbidden to discuss the research with colleagues or island residents.*

*Forbidden to disclose any details whatsoever of the research, including in letters, which shall be inspected, censored, and redacted, with the sender's address modified to leave no credible trace.*

With no other choice, Thomas signed each document with a trembling hand. The Major had one final thing to say.

'If you ever speak of any of this, people could die.'

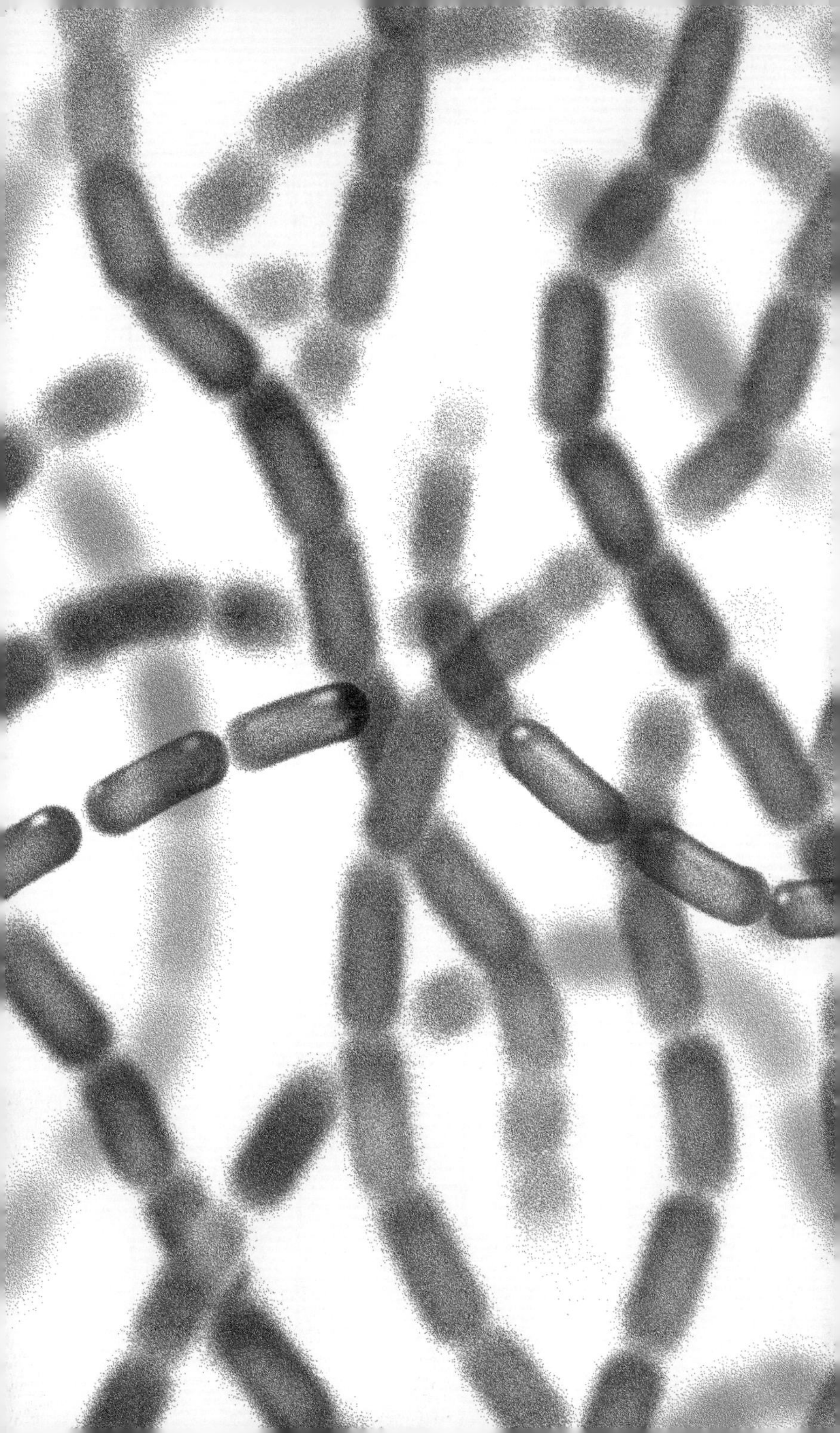

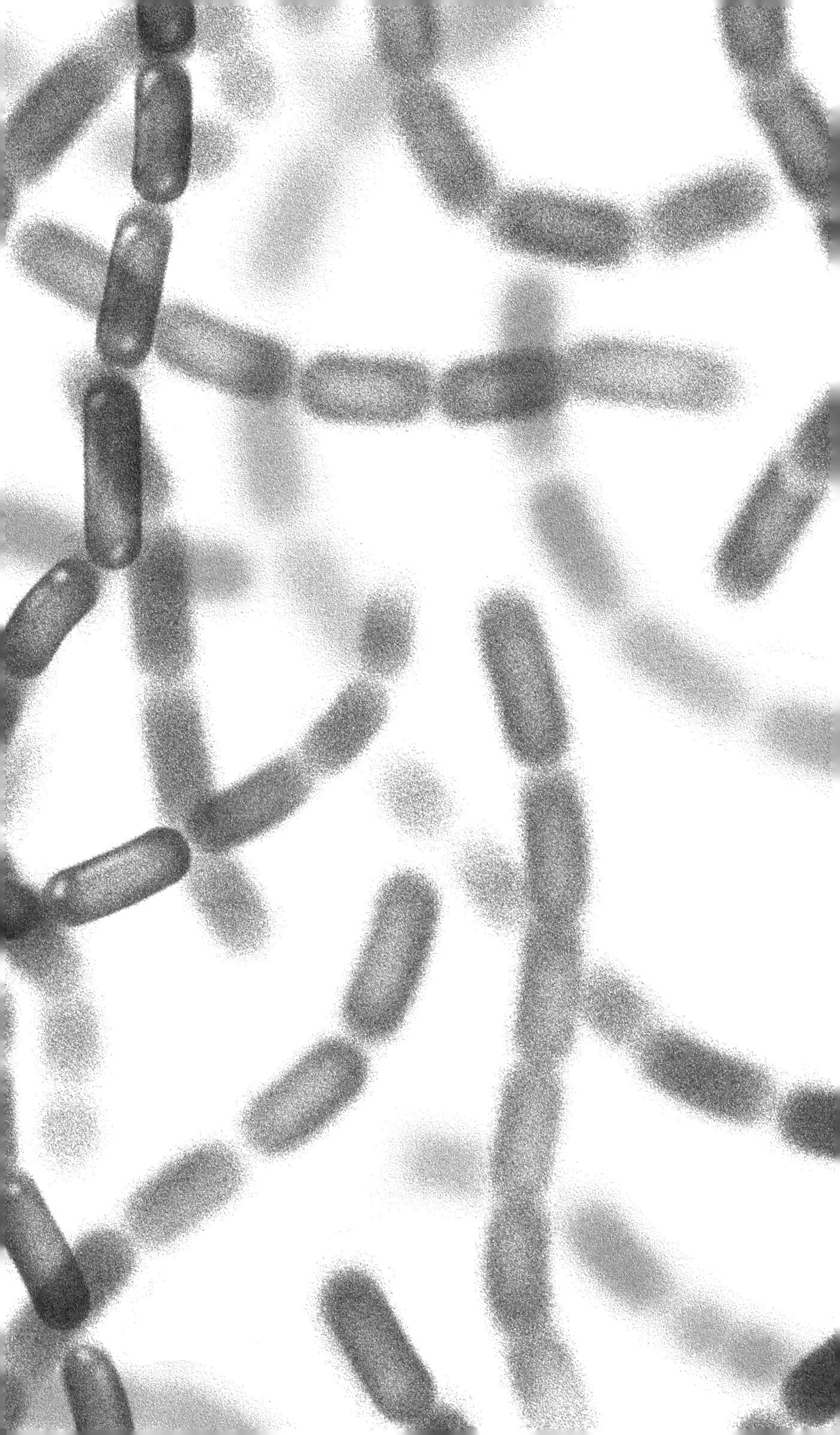

## HEAT WAVE

I doubt that you remember being born. Few species can. But I do. I remember every minute detail and each microsecond. Perhaps because my lifespan is so short, a few weeks at the very most; my memory is infallible. I flash back effortlessly, unspool my past at will in a vivid procession of faithful images and lossless smells. I can even travel back before my birth, as though my mother and hers before her passed down to me a portion of their memories as they brought me into this world.

I was born in the heat wave of mid-June 2025. The one that shattered every record from the twentieth century. A heat dome hung over Quebec, the temperature hadn't dropped below 30° Celsius for days, and daytime peaks were hitting 48°. There was nothing for people to do except burrow away in their basements or any available shade and wait for rain or milder weather. Those who had lacked the foresight to procure cold-air machines before they were all gone kept their windows thrown wide open or killed time at the water's edge, to our delight. You avoided all contact of skin against moist skin, only rarely giving yourselves over to the pleasures of the flesh.

Some meteorologists considered this intense dry heat irrefutable proof of climate change. Others called it a return to normal after months of heavy rains and snows. And Quebec did record 296.6 millimetres of precipitation, after 132.8 millimetres the previous year. Mother Nature had at last decided to dry out her sodden, wrinkled skin, to the detriment of harvests, water tables, lakes, and families crammed into high-rises.

For us, though, the conditions for fruitful reproduction were all in place. I came into the world during that heat wave, on the tidal flats of the St. Lawrence River. My mother and thousands of her kind laid eggs in dense pockets near the river. Three days later, I hatched alongside my hundreds of brothers and sisters. As callow larvae, we slid down the stem we were laid on and moulted three times. After the third instar, we sunk into the ground to pupate and remained there two weeks. As one, we entered our imago stage, mature enough now to take our own nourishment from the microorganisms in the sand. Your stomach would have turned at the sight of us cresting the banks of the St. Lawrence: a swarm of horseflies, moving as one sombre, voracious mass, caressing the tall grasses at sunrise.

# MARGUERITE'S HANDS

The first five minutes at the factory are always the most excruciating, a torture with no end in sight. On his seat in front of the hydraulic machine, Theodore tirelessly repeats the same movements. Stretch out the left arm, like a metal claw. Grab a spring from the tray. Twist the arm forty-five degrees, clockwise. Set the unit flush in its socket. Gently place both index fingers on the heat sensors to activate the mechanism. Watch as the machine tests the spring. Commit to memory the stiffness coefficient on the screen. Remove the spring with the right hand. Pivot the arms forty-five degrees, always clockwise. Place the coil in the funnel that will drop it into the correct box based on its measured resistance. Throw it out if defective. Repeat the cycle one thousand times per day, two thousand for a double shift.

At the start of each shift, Theodore's body revolts, twists and turns, bends over backward in desperate pursuit of the comfortable position that ever eludes him. His mind too is aflutter, in search of a tenable mental attitude. Ideas scattering, neurons firing. A heavy feeling overwhelms him, like an oxygen tank ready to explode the moment the atmospheric pressure climbs too high. A prisoner in his ergonomic seat, Theodore senses the full futility of his existence, his uselessness and insignificance and emptiness. A stiffness takes hold of his shoulders, neck, and arms. A fist closes around his ribs. The air supply grows scarce. Blood pulses in his temples, thumping the walls of his skull. His jaw locks. He must fight with every ounce of strength he has to hold back the anger gripping his insides, rising up and entwining his spinal cord all the way up to his throat. A voice in his brain screams: *Get up! Save yourself from this sorry excuse for a life!* But Theodore remains seated, paralyzed, robotically executing his movements. He closes his eyes. Listens to the ambient noise. Gradually, the drone of the nearby machines and the grinding and the motors, the hollering and the welding and the radio resolve in Theodore's head into some semblance of a melody. Once dialled in, each of these notes tunes right into the frequency of his malaise. Then he feels on the verge of fully disappearing into himself. From a distance he could be mistaken for just one more machine, an empty metal enclosure spinning endlessly around like a turbine on its shaft.

Yet today Theodore feels somehow unable to enter into his routine, always a fraction of a second behind the machines. The atmosphere is electric, the heat suffocating. The horseflies are throwing off his concentration. Two in particular have noticed his arrival and are tormenting him mercilessly. The burning of his bites from earlier that morning make it hard to stay calm. They've swollen up and his skin is breaking out in a painful rash. Try as he might to shoo them away, to catch and squash them, Theodore fails. It's as if they are too smart for him, anticipating his every swat. They make him nervous. He's sweating more than usual. He tries to check his rising anger, but he knows himself all too well. He can see his patience is frayed to the breaking point, feel himself slowing the pace of the line. When he has to place his fingers on the heat sensors, he can't lift them off fast enough to shoo a fly: if contact is broken prematurely, the machine reverts to its previous position and he has to start all over again. When that happens, two precious seconds are lost before he can start up the machine again. He'll clearly never make his quota if these awful creatures won't let him be.

All around the factory, the other employees are keyed up as well. They're stopping by each other's stations, chatting away, unconcerned that their actions will disrupt the rhythm of production. The mere thought of this laxity infuriates him. He watches them, sharing videos on their smartphones, slapping their thighs. Theodore doesn't get it. Why would they want to be constantly barraged by images? Just the thought of it fills him with angst. Thousands of eyes open as one and scrutinize him from head to toe. Just when he feels like he is going to explode, the foreman comes on the intercom. This does not happen often. All the employees stop what they are doing and look up at the ceiling, as if searching for an astral spectre.

> We have noticed horseflies in the factory. We will soon be closing the main doors and bringing you fly strips to stick around your stations. We are also aware of the extreme heat. The eight fans left in the office will be distributed to employees on the floor, with priority given to those nearest the ovens. Please carry on working as normal. And have a great day!

Theodore has worked at the spring factory over a decade, long enough to know that closing the doors does not bode well. The temperature will shoot up. The lack of light and air will be crushing. Stifling. Suffocating. The workers will be on edge. And then everything will go sideways. It always does, here. The workers can't keep their emotions in check, the noise and the machines have taken everything they have to give. Last time it got this hot, the foreman had to break up two guys fighting over the last Coke in the vending machine. A spattering of blood was left on the break-room walls.

If there is one thing Theodore hates above all else, it's confrontation. He has never been able to handle it. He'd rather hide away in his hole. Not make waves. Hug the wall. Let it pass. That's why, unlike the other workers, he never asks to change stations. Although he knows how to do every job in the factory, having tried each one at least once, Theodore is back at the torqueing machine, the station everyone else avoids because it's so repetitive. Above all, it puts him next to Marguerite. She is one of the only women at the factory. Her job is to untangle the springs. Theodore has long harboured the desire to ask Marguerite out, but he can't summon the words. In every facet of his life, he has only ever spoken when it was strictly necessary. From birth, he has felt himself to possess only a limited store of words. Social niceties don't interest him. He can never figure out what to say to come across as a regular guy. What mask to wear so as not to stick out. When people give him a cursory greeting, he never smiles back, just nods slightly and looks away, as if his attention has been suddenly called elsewhere. Over time, the other workers have grown used to him and stopped wasting their breath.

But not Marguerite: she keeps saying hello. It twists Theodore's bones into knots from the inside. He wonders if her hands are soft; his own are rough as sandpaper. He sneaks sideways glances at Marguerite, lingering over her busy fingers. Her skin, like his, is bluish on her forearms. He's noticed that she dislikes the sight of her dirty palms. A look of disgust sweeps over her face, and she pulls out a bag of lemon-scented wipes and painstakingly cleans her fingers, one at a time, scrubbing hard. The dust from the springs collects on your skin, it's true, colouring in the grooves like a fungus blossoming before your eyes. In less than an hour your hands are fully covered, and from there it spreads to your forearms and beyond. At first Theodore also found this hard to take. But he has gotten used to it; given enough time, he'll get used to anything.

Though Theodore now keeps a low profile, there have been missteps in the past. He remembers it like yesterday. The alienation of seventy-hour weeks can take people to some dark places. To make the time pass faster, he had assigned himself an hourly quota and would let his mind play scenes from an imaginary war. Hit your number and get the chance to thwart your enemy; miss it and the opposite occurs. After Theodore had worked for two days at this frantic pace, his foreman had to place him on forced leave. He'd become unresponsive to outside stimuli. Of course, after some rest, Theodore got back in the saddle, returned to his habits. But he had never been quite the same again. He was terrified by the latent fury he had glimpsed inside himself. Experience has taught him that there are certain things his nerves can't handle. He takes care not to cross the line. And a case of beer does the job when it's time to forget.

Since the incident, Theodore's psychotic episodes have been much milder. He sometimes imagines himself as a roll of steel arriving at the factory. His body is unrolled and flattened by a machine that swallows him up and turns him into springs. He then undergoes an array of treatments to increase resistance to fatigue and protect against corrosion. At the end of the cycle, Marguerite, who has been specially trained for the job, performs quality control. Methodically she untangles all his parts and delicately lines them up in the correct order. As she conducts her inspection, her bare hands touch each and every part of him.

'You doing a double tonight?'

Marguerite's question snaps him out of his reverie. Theodore hadn't seen her come over. She's even prettier up close. As he scrambles torturously for a fitting answer, she hands him three rolls of flypaper. It seems to him that he feels her smooth skin graze his.

'You should hang these up, Theo. It's gonna be a long day.'

'Thanks!'

'Did you hear the news? Scary, huh?' she asks, taking out her phone to show him the headlines of the hour.

'What?'

'All the domestic violence, in Berthier. Arrests in Montmagny.'

'Oh, that, yeah.'

'Kinda weird, right?'

Theodore doesn't answer.

'Did you hear what they're saying?'

'No, what?'

'Apparently they want to replace us. With a machine. You know what that means?'

Unsure what to say, Theodore lets the awkward silence settle in. Marguerite waits awhile, then goes back to her station, visibly disappointed by his unresponsiveness. Her platinum blond hair brushes her shoulders to the rhythm of her quick steps. Theodore shivers. The melody of her voice sticks in Theodore's head, overpowering the hum of the machines for many long minutes until he too slips off into space. A lemon scent hangs in the air: the smell of Marguerite's hands. One by one he unrolls the fly strips and hangs them up around his station. When she sees him doing it, she shoots him a smile.

# PROJECTS N, R, AND F

*July 15–August 3, 1942*

As soon as they arrived, Thomas and the other scientists were put up in one of three large hotel-like buildings on the west side of the island. Dozens of rooms had been prepared for them. Each had one window, one bed, one chair, one sink, and one light bulb. In appearance, at least, the scientists had everything they needed for a comfortable stay. Upon closer inspection, Thomas's quarters seemed more like a prison cell.

The first nights felt like an eternity. Thomas was kept awake by the stifling heat and the incessant drone of the insects trapped in the labyrinthine building. Their buzzing was hypnotic, countless thrumming, rustling wings and a raspy wheezing, sometimes high-pitched and sometimes deep, sometimes fast and sometimes slow. He lay in his bunk and watched the hours pass one by one. Thomas couldn't keep his mind from trying to associate these creatures' sounds with the images in his encyclopedia. But it was a lost cause with such a great variety of stridulations. The sun rising over the horizon came as a relief.

Each morning at seven, including Sundays, a ringing bell informed Thomas that breakfast was ready. He would get dressed and go down to the dining hall, a large open room on the main floor full of tables and chairs, with windows looking out toward the bay. The researchers and soldiers would gather there to eat. Colleagues traded furtive looks but few words; the scientists were under constant surveillance, especially by Major Walker, who paced around the room, enforcing silence.

Thomas soon realized that he was the only French-speaking scientist. The rest spoke to each other exclusively in English. Out of homesickness or affinity based on their shared language, he became fast friends with the islanders, some of whom were also being housed in the western sector. The army had hired a few locals as handymen and charwomen. In consideration of this service, they were allowed to remain on their island.

Thomas was especially fond of one islander, Rachelle, a blond woman in her twenties whose husband had recently enlisted in the air force. She reminded Thomas of his mother. Rachelle cooked the meals and cleaned the rooms. She enjoyed Thomas's discreet conversation, and in return offered him extra helpings of food. From Rachelle he learned an important piece of information: their location. Grosse Île had until recently been a quarantine station for immigrants arriving at the Port of Quebec City. Thomas remembered reading a story about it in the newspaper. Rachelle also explained that the scientists were sleeping in the first-class hotel, where only the most well-heeled immigrants had stayed. The soldiers bunked in dormitories in the second- and third-class hotels. He was not, she whispered, under any circumstances, to go walking in the fields to the east of the stable. That was where the migrants who perished were buried in mass graves. The soil was loose in places.

There was also a family of four young men and their father, who saw to various odd jobs for Major Walker. They took their orders from three NCOs who spoke basic French. When they weren't doing repairs in the buildings, they were stoking the boilers in the generator station, delivering the mail they brought over from the army base across the river, or looking after the animals. They were also tasked with ferrying people and goods to and fro, by canoe, even in winter. Men of few words, all save the youngest, Émeril, who couldn't have been more than sixteen. Thomas especially enjoyed this young man's company, and sometimes gleaned interesting tidbits about the mission in exchange for cigarettes.

All the scientists were dying to learn more about what was happening on the island, and Thomas was no exception. The army was keeping them in the dark about the research they'd been brought here to conduct. No one knew much beyond the little Major Walker had told them when they arrived: the biological warfare program on the island was a joint effort between the United States, Britain, and Canada; the top brass in Washington was keeping a close eye on their progress.

The island was divided into three sections. To the west, in the hangar by the docks, ten anthrax experts were assigned to Project N (for *Anthrax*). The objective was to produce 25 kilograms of anthrax weekly, which could be used to make 1,500 bombs. When Major Walker mentioned the number, everyone held their breath, starting with Thomas. He couldn't stop himself from thinking about how many lives might be lost as a result of their labour. After a year at that rate of production, the numbers got truly horrifying.

A little further north, to the right of the stable, was Project R (for *Rinderpest*), working to find a vaccine for the cattle plague and produce it in sufficient quantities to be ready if Germany attacked the Allied herds. As one of the biggest producers of food for the front, Canada was probably already in their sights. Fifteen virologists were working in rotating shifts, spurred on by Major Walker, who regularly reminded them that an attack could come at any moment, with catastrophic effects on the outcome of the war.

Lastly, to the east, in a house that had served as a lab back when immigrants were quarantined on the island, was Project F (for *Fly*). The team included a virologist, a pathologist, two epidemiologists, and Thomas, the insect specialist. Their mission was to develop methods for propagating epidemics using insects. To accomplish this, they had been provided a collection of highly virulent strains of viruses, bacteria, parasites, and promising fungus species from around the world. By introducing the organisms into various insect species, the scientists could make them vectors of transmission for the chosen pathogens. Their lab, in the main room on the first floor, was fitted out with microscopes, vials, Bunsen burners, safety equipment, and a battery of animal cages inhabited by mice, rats, and monkeys. Strangely, no one had bothered to take down the frames hung by the islanders whose home this once was. Above the hearth, a photo of an unknown family; flanking the door, an embroidered angel to the right and a devil to the left, whose gaze the scientists did their best to avoid.

Thomas's role in Project F was a crucial one: collect the largest possible number of samples of the island's many insect species. This entailed first identifying and studying each species, and then recommending the one with the greatest potential to fulfill the mission. Major Walker had given him three weeks.

From the very first days, Thomas dove into his work. Grosse Île was a boundlessly rich ecosystem, a complex environment with coastline, woods, and farmlands. It was home to an astounding diversity of insect life. Thomas had never seen such natural abundance. He immediately identified a plethora of butterflies, dragonflies, beetles, mosquitoes, flies, bees, wasps, midges, and stink bugs, including native species not found in his encyclopedia.

No less astounding to Thomas was the flora. The island was home to the most nauseating plant he had ever smelled. It brought to mind stories he had heard from colleagues about the corpse flowers that grew only in Southeast Asia. To attract insects, this slender purple flower emits an odour redolent of putrefaction, fecal matter, vomit, and the rotting flesh so attractive to insects. When Thomas described his findings to Émeril, the islander's expression turned grave. In the strongest of terms, he urged Thomas never to return to that part of the island. The locals called it *the cemetery*. There were stories of people who spent time there coming back possessed by the devil, a notion that later made Thomas laugh to himself.

Much of his time was spent working near the marshlands that covered the northern sections of the island, where the malodorous plant grew thick. By day he tirelessly skirted the perimeter with the butterfly net he used to capture flying insects without injuring them. Come evening, he returned with a lantern, concentrating on the marshy spots and tidal flats. Drawn to the light, the insects flocked to Thomas as if he were a will-o'-the-wisp. Some nights he found himself swarmed by hundreds of fireflies, their flickering lights like a message in code he could never decipher. Somewhat more troublesome were the invertebrates living in the soil. To capture them, Thomas dug up batches of dirt that he took back to the lab to sift through. For crawling insects he buried containers with openings at or slightly above ground level and then waited for them to walk into his trap.

To an outside observer, this work may have looked relatively pleasant next to that of Thomas's colleagues, whose days were spent handling hazardous substances. In truth, it was gruelling. Day after day, night after night, the creatures he was studying crept up from all parts, tracking Thomas's movements and attacking him ruthlessly. He was covered in bites, scratching all day, inadvertently picking off scabs and mopping up the trickles of blood from his wounds before they had the chance to properly coagulate. The pain stole over his body incrementally, filling up his mental space until he could no longer think clearly. He had to be perpetually on guard. Nothing in the life he had known before had prepared him for this mission.

Thomas was born and raised in Montreal. What he knew of natural ecosystems came mostly from reading. His parents had almost never travelled with him; his summers were spent with his nose in a book at the library. Before coming to this island, he had never witnessed the full scope of nature's violence, intensity, beauty, sweetness, aridity, and intelligence, all in the service of survival. Now, out in this wilderness, Thomas felt more like prey than predator. One family of flies in particular had been ferociously attacking him since he set foot on the island: *Tabadinae*. Without fail, one or two or three specimens would appear the moment Thomas approached a thicket of trees or the shoreline. It was as if they could sense his presence from kilometres away. Their triangular wings made them easy to identify. At first they would encircle him, testing his patience. Émeril simply called them horseflies and warned Thomas to never let them land on him. Their bite hurt like a punch to the face. But it soon became clear that there was no avoiding them.

Despite himself, Thomas had become fascinated with these *Tabanidae*. He found himself subjecting them to a more thorough analysis than the other insects, carefully studying their behaviour, anatomy, hunting prowess, communication system, and reproductive rate. For days on end, he observed, dissected, and dismembered them by the dozens, pinning their body parts to a cork board to more easily study them with magnifying glass and microscope. Then he made accurate drawings, recording their particularities in his notebook.

Through careful observation, Thomas identified multiple species of biting flies on the island. The most common was the *Chrysops*, of average size, found mostly in the tidal flats. But there was another kind, encountered only in the wetlands. This species was not in Thomas's encyclopedia. He could easily distinguish it from the *Chrysops* by its much larger body. It had spots on its wings reminiscent of eyes, certainly an adaptation to frighten predators. This native variety reproduced in malodorous plants. Thomas was surprised to observe that it had a very different life cycle than that of the common horsefly, which lived around two years. According to his observations, this species, which he named *Tabanus flos cadaver*, has a lifespan closer to that of the common fly, in the order of fourteen days, likely due to the corpse flower's trait of wilting prematurely.

Thomas found this species even more promising than the *Chrysops*. He carried out multiple experiments to learn more about its behaviour, even going so far as to let a few bite him. When Émeril heard this, he thought Thomas had lost his mind. One of the flies landed on his face, right by his eye, and he'd let it stroll along uninterrupted. It had stopped right on his cheek and proceeded to rip off a huge chunk of flesh. Thomas could have sworn the creature had looked him in the eye before biting, as if it possessed a form of intelligence. That was when he knew that he had found the chosen species.

*August 4, 1942*

Around three weeks into his observation process, Thomas recommended that *Tabanus flos cadaver* be used to develop a biological weapon. His report notes that, despite their size, these flies were instinctually voracious, reproduced rapidly, and could travel great distances. Most importantly, the females required a more voluminous blood meal to procreate than other species. Major Walker accepted his proposal, and Thomas was dispatched to capture the greatest possible number of specimens before summer turned to fall.

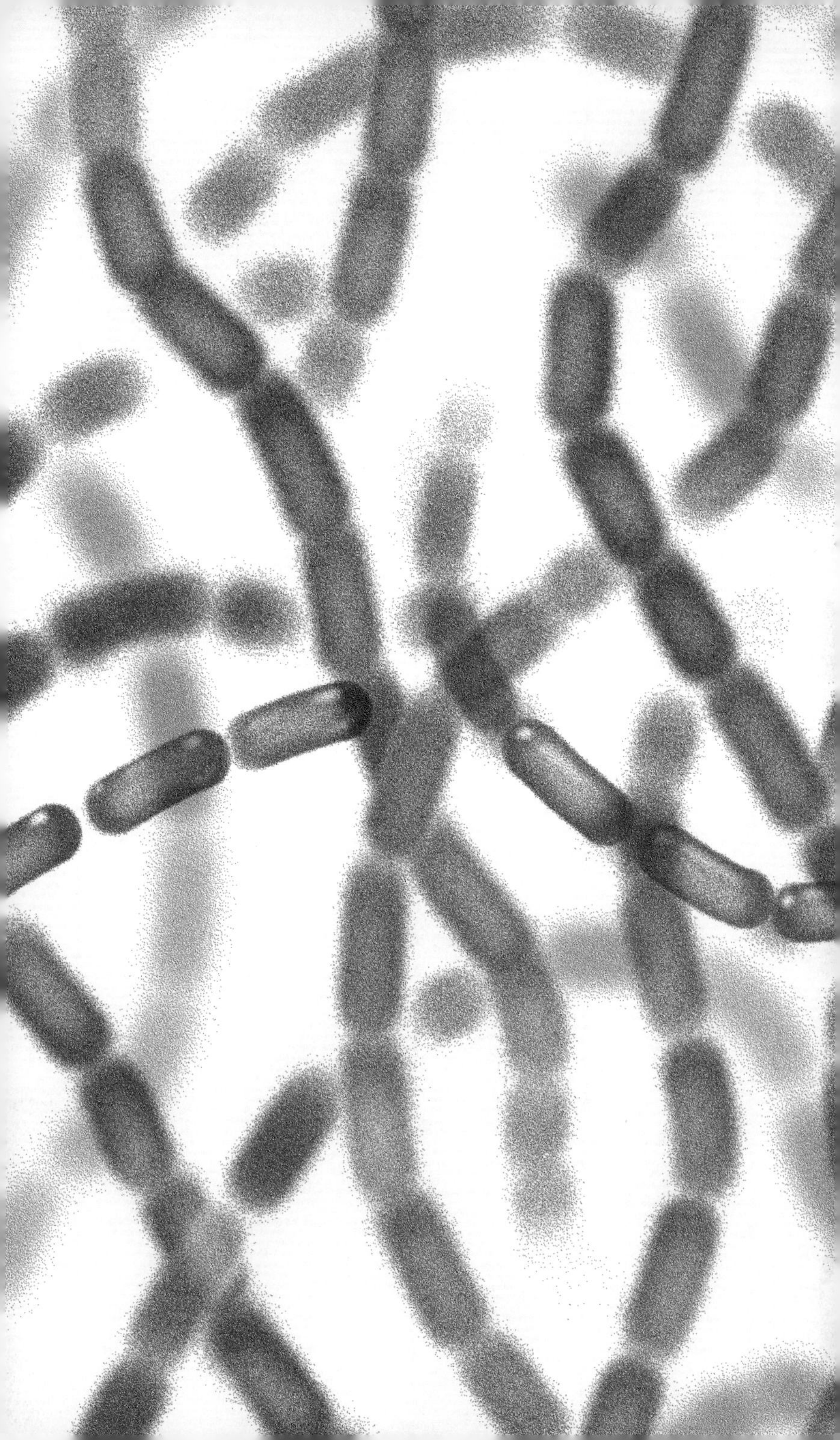

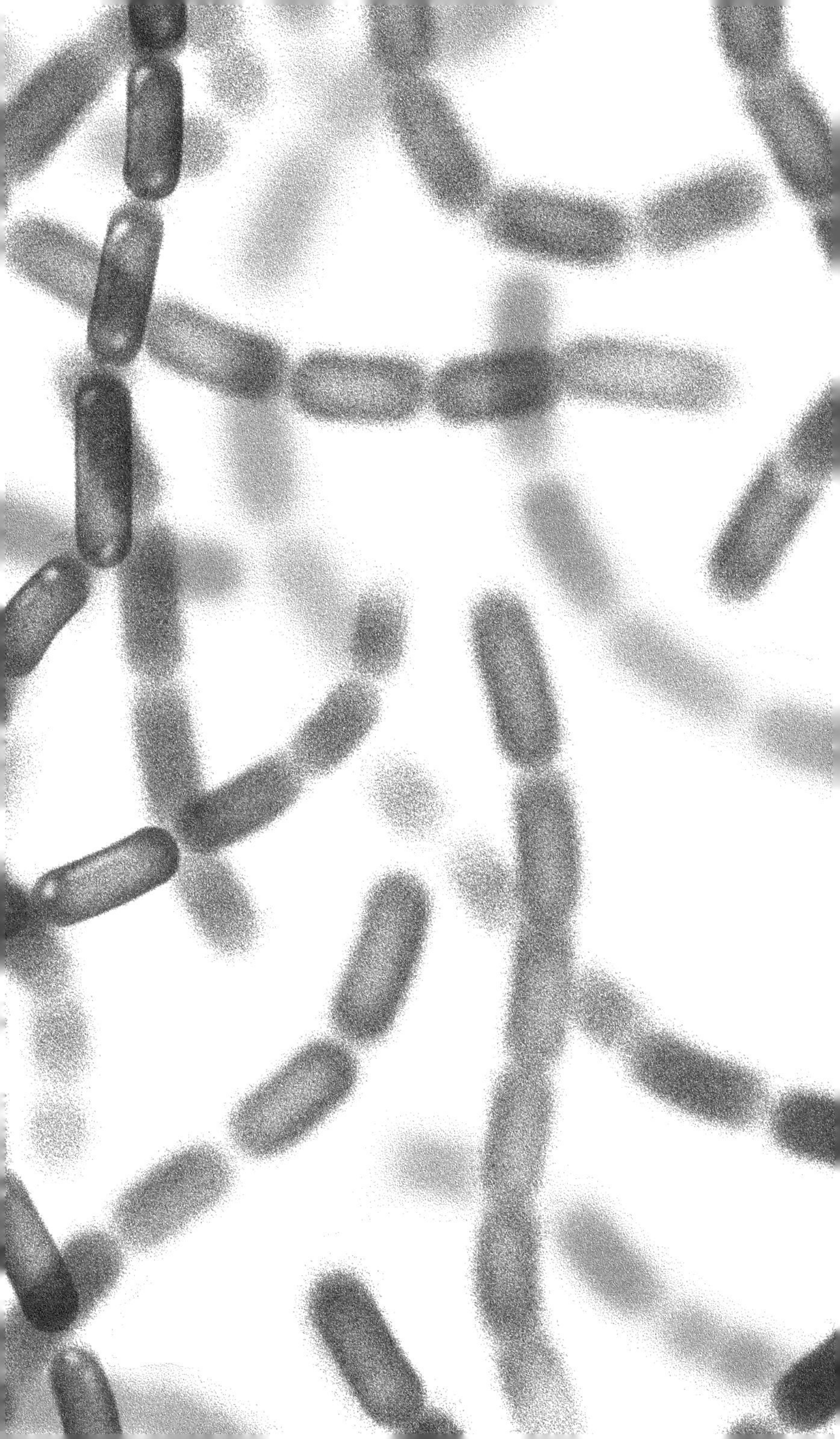

# BLOOD

Unlike you, we do not have the gift of speech. We communicate by dispersing chemical signals called pheromones into our environment. With these we send a panoply of messages to other members of our species: to attract sexual partners, mark our territory, signal nearby food or looming danger, and of course dissuade predators. With a little imagination, you might even conceive of us as a singular entity, a monad, and therein lies a strength of ours you could never lay claim to. You long ago lost all sense of the subtle congress between beings, which puts us at a great advantage.

Don't get me wrong. While we may have the capacity to communicate clearly, ours is a solitary nature. Mere hours after reaching maturity, we split off from the group. I began by exploring the environment into which I was born. I surveyed the tidal flats along the St. Lawrence River, touching the warm rocks and red sand, tall grasses and driftwood. I let myself drink in the gorgeous landscape. But there is no taming raw instinct. I quickly felt the need for hardier stuff than aphids. Our bloodlust is a matter of survival.

Most of my kind retreated to the fields where your cattle graze. I followed them out, and remained for a time, slaking my thirst. Day and night I fed on those hapless beasts, deftly outswerving their tails and inflicting on them a mild suffering of the kind only nature wreaks without remorse. Above all else I loved their tender ears. It was given to me to savour every inch of them, to stare into their anguished eyes in that fraction of a second when they felt the bite they were too late to escape.

I latched onto their heads and drank their thick warm blood. Sometimes it was my pleasure to delay my bite, to make sure they could feel my presence the moment I landed. It drove them wild and made me feel feverishly alive.

That was enough to keep me happy for a few days, as I did everything I could to avoid those of my kind, but animal blood proved – how can I put it? – not fully satisfying. Or was it perhaps the feebleness of their resistance to predators? One day, boredom drove me to follow the stable boy. Up to that point I had felt no particular attraction. A disagreeable smell came from him, especially his mouth with its white and malodorous curls of smoke. But that time, for some reason I can't name, his skin made my mouth water. I turned back and went into the stable. I tailed him between the empty stalls; the cows were all out in the fields. I almost let myself get sidetracked by my predilection for barn cats but caught myself in time. I stayed inside a moment, just barely time to fly out behind him before the door clacked shut. The young man strode toward the house next to the farm. It was sweltering. Drips of sweat beaded on his neck. Instinctively, I started circling. He noticed me almost immediately. Right when I was about to land on his glistening scalp, he ripped off his shirt and tried to whip me with it. I dodged it just in time and flew off, a few metres away. How striking the purity of that upper body, his smooth golden skin reflected in my eyes. I had never seen a half-naked man before. The sight alone was delicious, intoxicating. While I was lost in contemplation, the stable boy leapt into his car and closed the door before I could follow him in. I was left outside, looking in. White smoke poured forth from his orifices again. When he opened the window, I did not slip in through the crack. The air was too filthy. I let him get away, but swore that one day I would find among your kind an even choicer prey.

## GET ME OUT OF HERE!

Blunted by exhaustion, Theodore finishes his double shift and heads home. The sun has been up for at least three hours now. The night was hellish, the temperature refusing to drop by a single degree. He limply opens the fridge to grab a cold beer and chugs down half in one gulp. He has always loved this state of extenuation. After just one beer, he feels as if he's drunk a six-pack.

The radio plays a pop song. He knows the words by heart but can't figure out what they mean. Maybe nothing? His stomach grumbles, but Theodore just finishes his beer and cracks another. The news comes on the radio.

> The Montmagny police department is overwhelmed by the high volume of calls. The local authorities wish to remind the public to call 911 only in the event of a serious emergency. I repeat, do not call 911 unless you find yourself in a serious emergency.

Theodore walks around the apartment, bottle in hand, in search of something he can't name. He paces for minutes on end before the rank odour hits him. It can be smelled from every room, but seems to be coming from the kitchen. He walks over to the garbage can, disgusted. When he opens it, a dozen flies emerge, sprung at last from their trap.

'Jesus! How'd they get in there?'

He remembers the hole in the bedroom screen. He should have fixed it. The reek from the trash is pestilential, ripe as fish guts. His stomach turns. The horseflies are buzzing all over his apartment now. They seem bigger than normal, as if they fattened up while he was at work. As Theodore searches for a fly swatter, a blinking light draws his attention to the answering machine. Theodore aborts his mission and presses Play. It's the retirement home again. He lets out an exasperated sigh. It must be the fifth time this month.

As he listens to the nurse's message, Theodore stares for a long time at the machine. He feels a twinge of empathy, along with the crushing weight of the burden he has inherited. A massive fly lands in the corner of his eye. The mere thought of this creature suckling on his eyeball makes him slap himself in the face, hard. The horsefly dodges his blow and flees. Theodore groans. He'll have to get some traps. His thoughts turn to his grandfather. No, Theodore doesn't like the idea of them tying up his grandfather. He isn't a dog. No one deserves that. It's true that he wasn't the most affectionate surrogate father – gruff would be more like it. Still, he'd taken care of Theodore after the accident. Their relationship got trickier toward the end of their cohabitation, as Theodore grew less inclined to accept the old man telling him what to do. But despite it all, he held fond childhood memories. He'd liked living in the country, felt free there. Above all, he'd loved their hunting dogs. His grandfather always kept at least one in the backyard. A bone of contention between Theodore and his grandfather: Why couldn't the dog just sleep in the house?

'Dogs sleep outside. In the doghouse. End of story.'

One night, Theodore snuck out to keep the mutt company. After searching high and low, the old man found Theodore outside in the middle of the night and brought him back to bed without a scolding word. But for the next several days he'd made Theodore eat from the dog's bowl. For weeks he worked hard to drive home just how dangerous it was to trust animals. There was no telling what you might catch.

In Theodore's memories his grandfather often behaved erratically, angrily. Even with the best of intentions, he was always just slightly off-kilter. Theodore feels nostalgia stealing over him. He takes a last gulp of beer and dumps the dregs into the sink. He pulls a piece of jerky from the cupboard, grabs his car keys and the garbage bag, and leaves. He'll sleep when he gets home. Fixing the bug screen will have to wait.

It's a short drive. He reaches the retirement home before he has had time to properly chew his jerky. Theodore chose this residence for his grandfather because it was so close to his apartment. But often when he visits he feels like the drive goes too fast, like he doesn't have enough time to mentally prepare between leaving and arriving. Before cutting the engine, he turns on the radio to enjoy a few more moments of air conditioning. The host is still talking about the horsefly situation.

> Quebec government biologists arrived this morning to explore the shoreline of the St. Lawrence River for clues about what appears to be a massive hatching of horseflies in the region. Weather conditions in the past few years have …

Theodore is sick and tired of hearing people's opinions. Why can they never give a straight answer? Out of habit, he runs his wipers to scrape the windshield clean of dead insects, but now it's splattered with expansive smears of blood mixed in with a thick yellowish goop. Annoyed, he turns off the ignition and gets out. Before going through the main door he takes a deep breath and holds it in.

Theodore's hatred of this place is visceral. The idea of seeing people die has always made him squeamish. And what of the ascepticized fecal odour that hangs in the air, following you wherever you go? It ties his guts in knots. Once he gets safely home, it takes days to feel fully cleansed of it. As if the smell were clinging to him with razor-sharp claws. Just when he thinks he's tamed it with scented soaps, it comes back in full force. Now, as he himself nears the age when his parents lost their lives, every time Theodore draws near the hospice he feels a profound and nameless dread, a spiralling sense of foreboding. One day, he knows, it will colonize his entire being. Visiting his grandfather in his twilight years does nothing to assuage Theodore's anxiety. Death seems to be waiting around every corner in this place.

Theodore goes inside, mumbles his name at the front desk, then walks past the guard without stopping. As usual, he skips the elevator in favour of the stairs; he doesn't like enclosed spaces generally or this one in particular. He climbs all six flights without stopping. He's still out of breath when he slips into his grandfather's room. The old man is lying down, facing a window through which you can see the St. Lawrence River off in the distance. His wrists are bound. Tied to his bed, all he can see is the sky and the flies outside. One after another they crash into the window, each collision buzzing like an electrical impulse. Theodore walks over.

'Hi, Grandpa.'

But his grandfather doesn't answer. He's lost in his thoughts. Like Theodore, he has always been a man of few words, and good thing too, as far as Theodore is concerned. He walks around the bed and notices a redness on his grandfather's forearms. He must have fought back the previous night. Theodore grinds his teeth and loosens the straps. His grandfather sighs with relief and rubs his wrists. Once the old man's hands are freed, he takes a moment to gather his bearings, looking at Theodore. His gaze is glassy, shot through with fear – an expression Theodore knows all too well.

'Hi, Thomas. Long time no see. You're not working? Not on the island?'

For two years now, his grandfather has been calling him *Thomas*. At first, Theodore corrected him, but it made the old man so mad that he now prefers to play along.

'No. I came over on the boat this morning. To see you.'

Theodore's grandfather sits back down on his bed, somewhat reinvigorated. Theodore takes his arms and helps him stand up. The old man walks unsteadily toward the window. Theodore walks with him.

'See that skein of geese? Flying in on that strong easterly? They're flying real low. If I had my rifle, I'd get a few. My old dog never could sit still when they're coming in like that.'

Theodore smiles, reassures his grandfather that he'll bring him his rifle next time. The two men stare out at the horizon a few minutes, and then his grandfather asks to sit in the rocking chair. Once he is sitting, he stares at the TV hanging from the ceiling. It isn't on.

'Now why'd they go and hang that goose there?' he asks, pointing at the screen. 'It'll bleed out onto the ground, dirty the floor. Then the nurses will yell at me again. Are you gonna clean it? You can give it to the cook.'

Theodore sits down on the bed. He understands that his grandfather's memories sometimes play out before his eyes, in real time. Breaches have opened in his sense of time. To placate him, Theodore always plays along. The man who always seemed so vigorous has become positively frail. His beard is not trimmed. The remaining tufts of hair on his head are dirty, and some are sticking up in the air. His hospital gown is on backwards. His gnarled hands are shaking. He has gotten so thin that Theodore wonders how he can still stand up. His legs are like slender twin gun barrels, his cheekbones jut out from his hollowed-out cheeks. His stature is reduced as well, his body a hunched, shivery thing. Theodore often thinks that he now has the look of an aged hunting dog.

'Don't forget to take care of my dog before you leave. I don't want the others getting mad at me. They can't control themselves anymore. If you could see them! I'm worried.'

Theodore agrees with him, and gets up to go over to the bathroom. He comes back with his grandfather's old toiletries kit. Gently, he slides the rocker into the middle of the room, in line with the sink and mirror. His grandfather sees his own reflection but doesn't recognize himself.

'Who's that old man?'

Theodore doesn't answer. He slowly pulls the razor from the kit and sets it on the rim of the sink. He takes out a can of shaving cream and gives it a shake, shoots out just enough to fill his palm with foam. He runs the warm water and wets the razor. While he's getting ready to spread the shaving cream, his grandfather grabs his wrist. Theodore is startled. How, he wonders, can the old man still be so alert?

'I remember. They put up signs next to the mirrors. A picture of a man with an *X* over his mouth. They were in English, so I asked Thomas to translate. *If you say too much, this man could die.* So when you looked in the mirror, it was your own face you'd see. Get it?'

'What are you talking about?' asks Theodore, intrigued by this story.

His grandfather lets go of his wrist. 'Come on! Get on with it. What are you waiting for?'

Theodore tries to regain his composure as he lathers up his grandfather's cheeks, but the wheels in his mind are spinning freely. For years now, whenever his grandfather has spoken of the past, he has always been left to wonder where the old man's memory leaves off and his dementia begins. How much of what he says is true? When you get down to it, Theodore knows precious little about him.

'Quick, get me out of here! The Germans are coming!'

# LEAKS

*August 5–13, 1942*

Less than a month had passed when the first problems reared their heads. The officers were mired in a constant struggle to put out the little fires cropping up everywhere. Their strategy was threefold: limit contact between the scientists as much as possible, shroud any failures in secrecy, and keep the research in silos. But despite their best efforts at containment, rumours were getting around. The tension was palpable in every quarter, especially the dining hall. The scientists were on edge.

Thanks to what he had heard from Émeril and Rachelle, Thomas was unquestionably the best informed of his peers. Project R, he had learned, was getting nowhere. The scientists had found nothing concrete. To reduce the risk of contaminating their clothing, they had to do virtually all their work naked. Their skin was so red from antiseptic soaps that it was peeling off, to the consternation of Rachelle, who had to wash their sheets more often. Thomas had also learned from Émeril that the supply of lab animals was running very low. There were only a few head of cattle left. The next shipment was tied up in Quebec City, for reasons unknown.

The cattle were used by his Project R colleagues, who were testing new vaccines after injecting the cows with plague. Thomas sometimes heard the cattle lowing on his walk back from his nightly insect hunts. According to Émeril, most did not survive the tests. And it fell to Émeril and his brothers to euthanize the survivors, first hauling the bodies to the scientists for autopsy and then cremating them or burying them in mass graves near the stable. Émeril told Thomas how he loathed this work. It was an affront to common decency for someone like him, whose family had always scraped by on what the land provided. Thomas would have liked to explain a little better, but doubted his friend could have grasped what they were doing here. After all, he himself understood only a small part of it.

Project N was faring little better. The anthrax they produced was set out on trays and stored in the autoclaves formerly used to disinfect the belongings of quarantined immigrants. The equipment had never been updated. The autoclaves were in a deplorable state, clearly not airtight. According to Émeril, the scientists were handling the equipment with the greatest of care. The hangar doors had to be closed at all times, and everyone working wore gas masks and thick cotton coveralls. After being sent out three times to repair the windows and front door, Émeril knew first-hand the appalling conditions of the workers inside. Each time he'd gone in, he'd almost fainted in his stifling protective gear. The smell stuck to him, a mix of sweat and leather that made him feel as if his skin had been baked. Émeril had also told Thomas about an argument he'd witnessed between Major Walker and some of the scientists. The Major had smashed his fist into a table, wildly waved his arms around, and yelled. Émeril wasn't sure he fully understood why, but he believed the Major was upset because the research was taking longer than he wanted.

The Major's problems went beyond the outmoded facilities and slow pace of research. The unmanageable profusion of insects in the lab where anthrax was being manufactured raised concerns for both soldiers and scientists. Thomas had been privy to more than one guarded discussion over meals. He'd even heard that a telegram on the matter had been dispatched to Washington. The flies – horseflies in particular – got into every nook and cranny, door jambs and window frames and the researchers' clothing and the stores of provisions. They seemed to creep up out of nowhere, flitting around every which way, landing on the anthrax trays and then flying off before anyone could kill them or figure out where they were coming from.

*August 14–18, 1942*

Because cross-contamination levels were deemed unacceptably high, Major Walker sent Thomas into the hangar to find a solution. Washington's orders were clear: production must proceed apace, at any cost. It was the first time the Major had spoken directly to Thomas. Up close, the Major's eyes were so dark that his pupils appeared fully dilated. Thomas's first impression was that he resembled a falcon. Not wanting to vex the man, he set to work immediately.

The first order of business was to inspect the premises. The hangar's proximity to the tidal flats, the horseflies' main breeding ground, wasn't helping. The Major dismissed out of hand Thomas's recommendation to move the lab. The autoclaves' massive size, great weight, and poor state of repair made them liable to further deteriorate in transit. Thomas then asked for Émeril and his father's help to fix up the building as best they could, though it was foolish to imagine they might patch the cracks between every board. After two days it became clear that, try what they might, the horseflies would always find a new way in.

Thomas tried another tack, laying various types of flytraps. First, he installed large fine-meshed netting over the autoclaves, in the hope of catching the horseflies in flight. Next, he laid glue traps, spreading the resin in strategic areas of the anthrax production line and carefully placing chunks of meat or fish as bait. The second a fly landed on the gluey substance, it was caught. Some captured flies bit off their own feet and flew away; others died a few hours or days later. Thomas hoped, by these methods, to lower the risks of transmission.

*August 19, 1942*

A scientist in the first-class hotel was quarantined with a violent fever. Thomas heard the news from Rachelle. She had been asked to bring the man hot liquids every four hours, along with clean towels to switch out the previous batch, which she was to boil the second she got back. She was strictly forbidden from going near the infected.

*August 22, 1942*

A second scientist was placed in quarantine. Then Émeril and his brothers were called to take the two sick researchers across to the mainland. Major Walker insisted that they had to get to hospital in Quebec City in a matter of hours. In Émeril's telling, the scientists were a sorry sight. Both their bodies were covered in extremely painful-looking black carbuncles. One was delirious and running a high fever. In the low tide, the ferry couldn't reach the island. The soldiers had to strap the invalids onto stretchers, which were then tied down in the middle of a canoe. One by one, they were ferried across the river to a waiting military ambulance. The whole operation meant hours of rowing for Émeril and his brothers, who returned at dusk exhausted.

That evening in the dining hall, Thomas sat with an American researcher he'd spoken to in the Project N laboratory. Emboldened by the disarray that had taken hold since the two scientists' departure, Thomas questioned his colleague, who didn't hold back. He admitted, in a whisper, that the two men had undoubtedly contracted anthrax after coming into contact with spores. He didn't think they would be coming back; the infection had progressed too far.

Before being assigned to the island, Thomas had known little about *Bacillus anthracis* beyond a few mentions in university biology courses. So he was at once fascinated and terrified by what he learned from his American colleague. In a hostile environment such as soil, the bacillus could mutate into an endospore. Protected by a tough outer husk, these spores became exceptionally resistant to temperature variations, acidity, explosions, and even disinfectants. According to the researcher, cells could survive in their spores, without losing their properties, *for more than a century.* This was certainly why the Americans had singled it out for further research. Such a spore could make a formidable biological weapon. The scientist went on to detail the many forms infection could take. Symptoms varied based on the nature of the contact, but consistently appeared seven days after exposure.

Cutaneous infection anthrax – the form least dangerous to humans – is characterized by the formation of pruriginous itchy bumps like insect bites, followed by ulceration and the emergence of scabby eschars, black in colour and ringed by red or violet circles. If treated too late, infections can be fatal. This cutaneous anthrax was undoubtedly the form the scientists had caught.

A second form, gastrointestinal anthrax, is contracted by ingesting raw or undercooked meat from an infected animal. Symptoms include fever, shivers, swelling of the ganglions in the neck, abdominal pain, nausea, loss of appetite, vomiting, and diarrhea. With appropriate treatment, the odds of survival are high. In theory, this form was of least concern to the people on the island, as Major Walker had forbidden everyone from eating wild animals. But in practice it was less clear-cut. Thomas knew that Émeril and his family were ignoring the orders and illegally trapping in the forest. More than once he had caught them sneaking home with small game after nightfall. Despite multiple attempts to remind them of the importance of these orders, Thomas knew they still hadn't listened.

The last and deadliest type of infection, and the one most feared by the scientists, was inhalation anthrax. Inhaling anthrax spores is fatal. The first signs resemble a common cold: high fever, sore throat, generalized discomfort, muscle aches, fatigue, cough, chest pain, shortness of breath, fast heart rate, profuse sweating. This form can swiftly degenerate into pneumonia. Few survive more than forty-eight hours after the onset of symptoms. Beyond disinfecting wounds and administering anti-anthrax serums, there were few available treatments.

The scientist explaining all this suddenly stopped eating. He looked Thomas in the eye and admitted that his own greatest fear, which he shared with his colleagues, was never being sure whether they might have been exposed during their workday. Had they overlooked something while putting on or taking off their personal protective equipment? Had a fly slipped into their clothing after landing on a tray of anthrax? Could a spore have entered their bodies through their nose or mouth? There was no way to know for sure until several days had elapsed. Living with such a level of risk was, in his words, *a form of torture*. Thomas felt sorry for the man. Just when the scientist was about to add something further, he checked himself. He discreetly said goodbye to Thomas and left. The Major had entered the dining hall.

When Thomas got back to his room after the meal, he too examined his skin for suspect lesions. Every day from then on, he would religiously carry out the same series of checks, as if expecting the worst. Nothing was ever the same; nightmare after nightmare troubled his sleep. In them, he saw the bodies of the two contaminated scientists, burning with fever, slipping in between his sheets while he slept. He would wake up screaming, convinced he was being buried alive in a mass grave by Major Walker. Even the next day, he could not chase the lingering taste of dirt from his mouth. He was incapable of going back to sleep, his thoughts turning relentlessly back to the masses of people who could die from anthrax exposure if there were an explosion or serious leak. In strong winds, the weapon they were developing could infect everyone within a radius of several kilometres.

Up until then, Thomas had felt somehow spared from the broader horror. He had simply and dutifully gone about his business. This habit of thought may have been a survival instinct. But now that he understood the details, he felt like he had swallowed a colony of fungus that was eating away at him from the inside, digesting a little more of him each day. He feared that, given time, it would consume him entirely. War shifts our reality so that each individual action is perceived in isolation, rendering the most horrific crimes against humanity almost palatable. How did the other scientists and the soldiers live with the crushing burden? Did they ever look themselves in the mirror? As for Thomas, whenever he caught a glimpse of his face in a reflective surface, he saw his own terrified eyes. He imagined how his mother would look at him, or his father, in bafflement surely, laced with disappointment and shock at the sight of their son being swept up in this collective delirium.

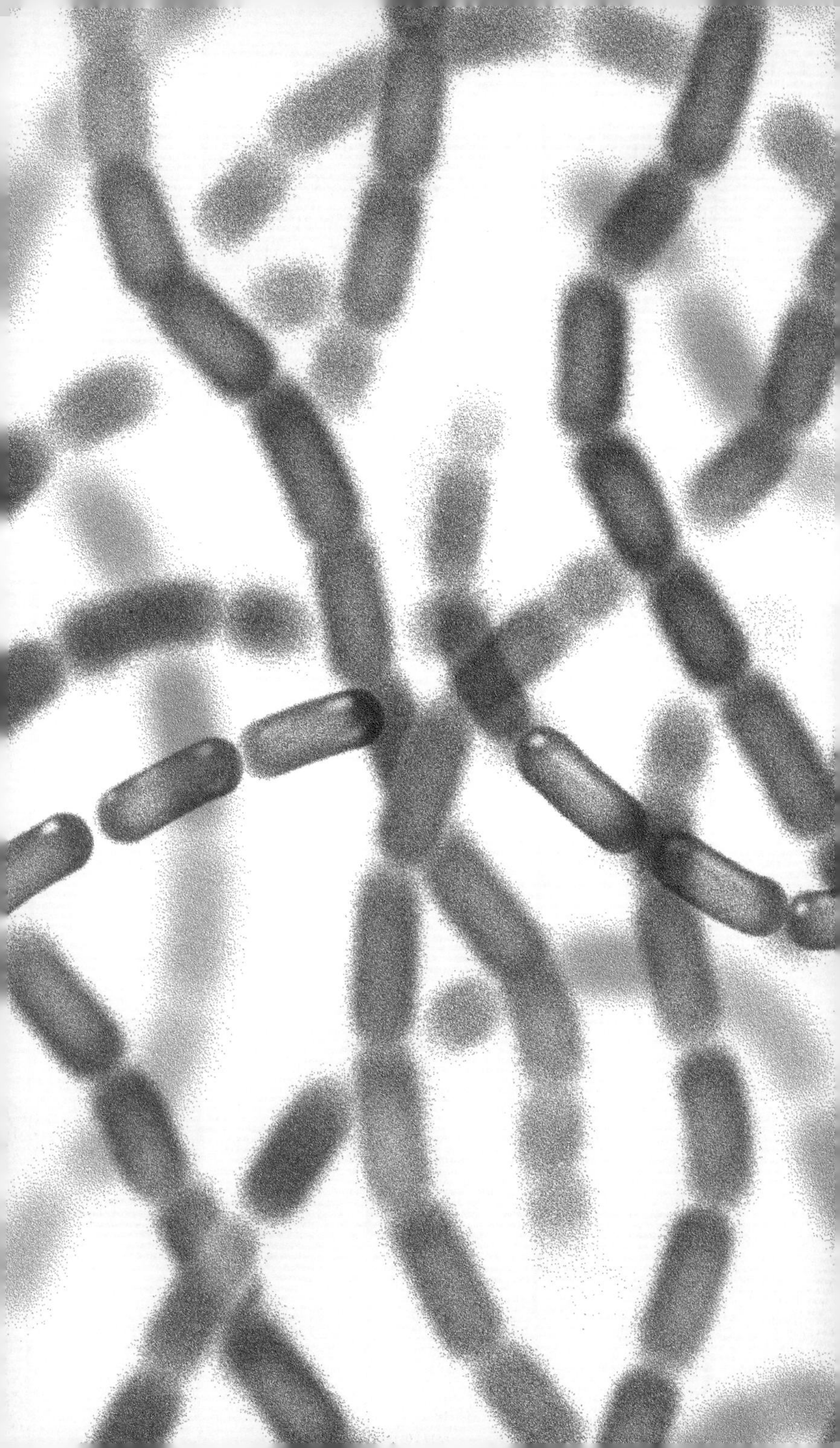

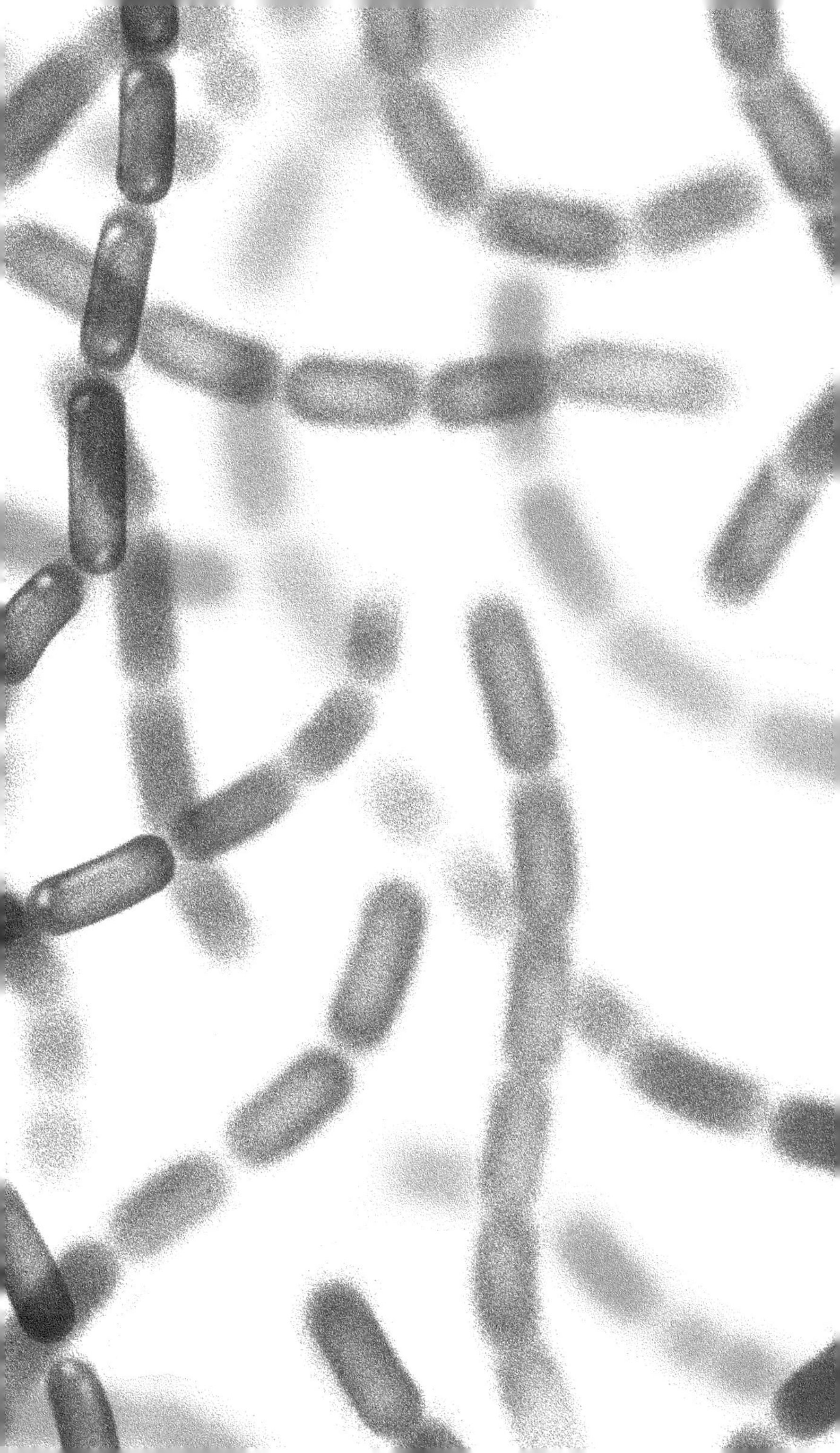

## EPIPHANY

As the heat wave settled in, I left the country for the city. Wherever I went I found ways to slip in, just one among hundreds of my kind. I visited all your favourite spots in turn, beginning with the most easily accessible, tents and trailers and cottages, and progressing to your open-windowed houses and apartments. I sampled different types of skin and flavours of blood and sweat, men and women and children, people sick and under stress, clean and dirty alike. I digested your flesh to achieve my aim of one day reproducing. So many bodies, yet not one came close to how I felt upon first glimpsing the skin of that farm boy. So I pursued my solitary wanderings, fleeing the other insects who were so plentiful that year.

Then one day, hotter even than the one before, I found myself flying over one of your neighbourhoods where I'd never been before. The doors of an enormous building were wide open, and I was sucked inside. The heat was stifling, a glorious sensation for one such as myself. You were all busy, united in toil. I flitted around from person to person with little real interest – until I found you. *You.*

Your kind is often unaware that horseflies see in colour. We can visualize up to two hundred images per second, enabling us to analyze your movements; for all intents and purposes, we can stretch out time. That's largely why you find it so hard to catch us. What I'm saying is that, the first moment I saw you, the cadence of the world around me slowed to a crawl. The machines, the people, the wind-pushing contraptions: everything receded to the background. All that remained was you, standing, and me, hovering above your head. The two of us, immobile in space. Your blond hair. Your eyes, set so deep in your face and of an almost verdant blue; your shoulders, muscular and knotted by labour; your hands, dextrous and powerful. An indescribable and uncontrollable intoxication gripped me. The first sign was a numbness in my feet. Next, a swaying, a coil of energy irradiating every portion of my being, to my mouth. I would have given anything to slip under your blue work shirt. Sashay in between two snaps. Touch down on your damp skin. Tasty. Salty. Warm. Unbeknownst to you, I'd parade along with my proboscis outstretched. I would taste each of your most intimate parts.

I stayed there a long time, watching you, sinking into a time lapse, delighting in this whirlwind of ecstasy. To check my instincts, I had to dig deep into my reserves of inner fortitude. This was neither the time nor the place to fulfill my desire. For that, I'd have to wait till we could be alone.

## BEFORE THE BITE

The moment he gets back from the retirement home, Theodore slumps onto his bed, overcome by a powerful languor. A scent of rotten flesh from his old trash can hangs over the kitchen. Disgusting. Flies are buzzing around every room, but he's too tired to fight them off. His burps smell of the hamburger he bought and shunted down his throat. It's noon, almost forty-eight hours since he last slept. Snatches of the news on the radio only add to his listlessness.

> Record highs all around Quebec ... 40° Celsius ... a high not seen since 2021 ... reports of four new violent incidents in Montmagny ... a fight at a local bar ... two men hospitalized ... no sign of wind or rain in the days ahead ...

Theodore's clothes cling to him like wings in the sun. He's tormented by thirst. His pinwheeling thoughts collect in a bottleneck. Little by little, a mirage casts itself over his sense of reality. A heavy black blanket covers his skin. His head throbs, but his limbs are numb. Dehydrated and confused, he replays that morning's scene with his grandfather on a loop. It ties his heart in knots. How much more time does the old man have left to live? At almost ninety-eight, he should be dead. It won't be long now, surely. What keeps him holding on? Theodore hopes the end comes soon. This is no way to live out his last days. It would have been better to let him die at home in the country, in Berthier-sur-Mer.

Theodore recalls how, before fully losing his bearings, his grandfather told him that he could feel his mind slipping off its rails.

'It's like I'm sitting in the theatre, watching a movie. I see things that aren't really happening – but I'm seeing them for real. I'm scared I'll never wake up.'

Theodore hadn't answered, but he made the decision to put his grandfather in a home. Now that the man has almost fully retreated behind a curtain of dementia, Theodore regrets not asking him more questions while his mind was still intact. The truth is that, other than the time they spent together over the years, Theodore knows nothing about his elder. What could he possibly have done, in his youth, to want so badly to keep it hidden away at any cost? When Theodore was younger, he sometimes tried to coax the odd story from him, but his grandfather sidestepped his questions or changed the subject every time. After a while, Theodore simply gave up.

Pushing down his deep sadness, Theodore falls asleep, a brick on the bottom of the river. The aseptic smell of the retirement home still clings to his clothing, so few horseflies will risk landing on him. The females are swirling around above his head, brushing against him, rising and falling, flying up and down in the air, salivating at the thought that he is right there – so close, yet inaccessible.

When Theodore opens his eyes it is already dark. The radio drones on in the background. A harrowing thirst torments him, and a burning itch: he examines his legs and finds two fresh bites, thinks of the fat flies that must have broken out of the garbage, of the still-unrepaired screen on his window. Theodore swears. The temperature still hasn't dropped a single degree. The clock reads 11:34 p.m; he doesn't start work until 3:00 p.m. the next day. It's going to be a long night. Theodore feels a gnawing hunger. In his room, huge horseflies are crashing into every surface, buzzing off the walls and ceilings, light fixtures, and furniture. He can't shake the feeling that one of them is going to penetrate one of his orifices at any moment.

He gets up, takes a shower, puts on clean clothes, scarfs down leftover pizza, and flees his apartment like a man slipping through the gates of hell. Outside is little better; not a wisp of air troubles the dome of stagnant heat. Instead of standing still and melting, Theodore takes a walk through the neighbourhood streets. He breathes a little easier. His feet fall into a steady pace, to the muffled sound of music from the neighbourhood bar. Before he realizes what he's doing, he finds himself at the front door. The bar is packed; it feels like the whole city is there. Shadows dance behind steamed-up windows. People seem to be having fun. Theodore imagines the cool conditioned air that must be cycling through the room. The mere thought of it gives him a lift. Without thinking it over, he goes inside. The cool air softly takes hold of his skin.

A disco ball above the dance floor grabs Theodore's attention. Thousands of rays of light splinter the room, illuminating the bodies for mere fractions of a second. A flash pierces his right eye, forcing his pupil to spontaneously contract before receding into the distance. The smells wash over him like waves. Synthetic and floral emanations mixed with the tang of sweat quicken his senses. He moves forward and stares at the men and women letting loose and rubbing up against each other, hot and bothered, packed in close and pressed against each other in an organic throng, like insects swarming over a body of water. Theodore isn't sure he fully understands the spectacle unfolding here before him, but feels an uncontrollable urge to move forward and join the crowd. He weaves his way to the centre of the dance floor, easing around women and shoving men out of his way. Once he's finally under the disco ball, he lets the music and the hands sweep over him. Although he has never liked dancing, he closes his eyes and abandons himself fully to the rhythms of the crowd. Any distinction between himself and the others breaks down. He moves like this for many long, delicious minutes, completely unburdened.

Then Theodore feels an altogether different hand running along his body with greater insistence. This contact makes him feel naked, stripped down to his bones. He struggles to reclaim his sense of himself, like swimming upstream. The fingers have now slipped in under his shirt and are lustfully stroking his stomach and pecs. The skin is marvellously soft. He feels the nails digging into his flesh, sending a long shiver through his body. His abdominal muscles contract. An untenable tension gathers in the seat of his desire. In a synchronized pulsing, it pistons up to his heart and back down, again and again. Theodore opens his arms. The ball of energy expands outward, encircling the two of them, pulling them together. Their breathing quickens. With eyes still shut, he places the backs of his hands on the woman's bare shoulders, delicately sliding them along her arms down to her fingers. He joins his palms to hers, clasps them there. A bolt of heat pierces him. Next, he lets his hands survey the hollows at the sides of her rib cage. Her skin is so soft. He clutches her more tightly. Animal impulses slip their fetters. Desire swells. The woman's hands now travel down between Theodore's legs, where the blood is gathering. Theodore grips the woman's pelvis and feels desire cresting like a wave. Unable to stand it another moment, he opens his eyes.

Somewhere inside he had known it was her from the start. He takes her by the hand and drags her to the exit. They rush to his place without a word. The moment the door closes behind him, he picks her up and leads her to the bedroom, where he starts kissing her mouth and cheeks, her chin and lips, her breasts and stomach and thighs; he bites her, gently at first, and then harder. She quivers. In the sultry heat they take off their clothes and bring their bodies together until the moment of climax when, as her teeth dig into Theodore's shoulder, Marguerite comes and Theodore does too. Stirred by the intensity of it all, he doesn't notice a fresh fly bite behind his ear.

# THE ERROR

*August 23–September 4, 1942*

The summer had slipped Thomas by in the blink of an eye. The bluish circles under his eyes betrayed his fretful nights. Despite Rachelle's attentions, he had lost weight in recent weeks. He hoped his mother would never see him in this state. The nights now grew cooler the moment the sun slipped over the horizon. The insects were falling silent, preparing for diapause. Like a lull in the tide, a state of waiting crystallized, a tangible stillness engulfing the island.

Thomas was now working at the lab around the clock. They had injected the horseflies with a selection of viruses and bacteria, influenza and plague and brucellosis and typhus, but successful transmission to a lab rat had yet to occur. The quantity of specimens Thomas gathered in the mud flats was never enough to meet his colleagues' daily needs. So with Émeril's help, he had drawn up plans for a breeding pen for *Tabanus flos cadaver*. Thomas had him build ten boxes with ventilated covers to house one hundred of the wild horseflies he had captured. On each box they wrote key information and dates pertaining to the tests. Thomas paid closer attention to the females than the males. Inside the containers, a nutrient-rich environment had been created, and new vermin were thrown into the boxes every three or four days to give them the blood meal needed to reproduce. To recreate the mud flats, the vivaria were filled with sedge and sphagnum, rushes and aphids and corpse flowers. The temperature was kept constant at 28°C, humidity at 68 per cent. Each day Thomas monitored his habitats, adjusting one variable at a time, in the hope that the horseflies would soon breed.

*September 16–24, 1942*

After two weeks of waiting, a gelatinous glop appeared in the heart of a flower. Delicately, Thomas placed the hundred eggs in a new box. Five days later, the first larvae hatched. Then, after two further weeks of waiting, some of them pupated into flies. Thomas could not contain his cry of joy. Thanks to this new generation of subjects, laboratory research could now move forward, though Major Walker forbade the scientists from telling anyone of even the slightest success. He was spending more and more time with the Project F scientists, heartened by their incremental progress. He relentlessly exhorted them to go faster, skip steps, begin testing on rats – all in the hope of having something concrete to report; in Washington, patience was wearing thin.

*September 25–November 24, 1942*

One morning on the way to his lab, Thomas felt the year's first chill on his face. Suddenly the dew froze his toes. The following day, the sky filled with thousands of white geese, famished from their long migration. Like an apparition, the flocks invaded every inch of Grosse Île's shoreline, thrusting their long necks into the clay-rich soil to eat the roots of the rushes. The buzzing of insects gave way to the squawks of wild birds. Finding rest became harder than ever. While he and the other scientists lived in the strictest possible isolation and under tight military guard, these geese were out gallivanting day and night. The irksome honking of their conversation was leaching into even Thomas's smallest thoughts.

Thomas was surprised to find that he envied these birds. He resented their freedom, the very freedom that had been stripped from him the moment he landed on this island. Especially at night, he stared out his room's tiny window at the geese in peaceful repose, letting themselves be tossed around along the shoreline, out of their predators' reach. The moon's rays reflected off their white plumage. At times like these, Thomas had the sense that he was witnessing flocks of ghosts that had lost their way along their journey from another time. Never had he known anything quite like this feeling of being on the flight path of creatures in motion, yet unable to follow them. He missed his old life. Would he ever get it back? And if he did, what state would he be in?

On windy days, Thomas thought of Émeril and his brothers. He hoped against hope that they hadn't responded to Grosse Île's hunting ban by taking their rifles elsewhere on the archipelago. Thomas pictured them coming home with geese slung over their shoulders, held by their long necks, riddled with lead shot and contaminated with anthrax. The thought made his throat clench and he could barely swallow, as if choking on the secret he was struggling to hold inside.

Thomas had developed a sincere respect for Émeril and his family, with whom he had worked closely since arriving on the island. It was getting harder and harder to lie to them. But he knew all too well that if a soldier figured out that they had information on the research, they ran the risk of being interrogated or even taken as prisoners of war. And that Thomas did not under any circumstances want to imagine.

*November 25–December 15, 1942*

The first snow had fallen, the geese had ventured southward in a cannonade of beating wings. Thomas awoke one day and they were gone.

Total silence fell over the island. The absence of sound was even harder to bear than the noise. Nature slowed to a standstill, the earth and clay compacted, the river's surface took on a creamy smoothness, the frazil clung to the banks like beads on a rosary. A sheet of ice began to form, thin as glass at first and then gradually thickening into a proper layer of sea ice, impenetrable to waves. Even Rachelle had stopped smiling. She knew no one would make it through winter unscathed. The tides kept on rising and falling as the cold set in to stay, and four weeks later the metamorphosis was complete.

*January 2, 1943*

Thomas had just crossed over into sleep when he was jerked awake by a sharp knock on the door. Before he could get up, he saw Émeril rushing to his bedside. The young man looked ghostly in the darkness. He put a finger on Thomas's lips and a hand on his chest. His eyes were red and wild; he was shaky, deranged, wracked by muscle spasms and reeking of sweat. Thomas's survival instinct kicked in and he worked himself free, which gave Émeril a minute to recover. He stood up straight in the middle of the room.

'Help me,' Émeril begged.

Thomas bounded out of bed. His heart was pounding. He gave Émeril a signal – *stop talking* – and threw on some clothes. So as not to wake the other scientists, he whispered to Émeril to meet him in the laboratory. Émeril left first; Thomas followed behind. Deep in the night, under the gleam of an enhaloed moon, the island looked hostile. A glacial northeasterly whiffled their cheeks and whipped the snow into fine powder. In his haste, Émeril tripped several times on the ice pellets scattered over the frozen roadway. He was not ordinarily this clumsy. Thomas followed him. He was worried. Once he reached the laboratory, Émeril climbed the steps two by two and pushed inside. Right behind him, Thomas closed the door and turned on the lights. The two men looked each other in the eye. Émeril spoke first.

'I don't know what's happening to me. I think I made a mistake.'

Thomas tried to calm him down by sitting him on the central table. After making him take a deep breath, he asked Émeril to explain, in detail and above all slowly, what had happened. Émeril nodded, then went through the events of the last twenty-four hours.

***19:20.*** *Émeril had finally finished making the new breeding pen. He was to bring it to the lab that evening. When he got there, the scientists were already back at the hotel. He lay* *the box down on the counter but did not leave right away. He inspected the condition of the ten boxes he had already built. Each held around twenty horseflies. He noticed that the holes in one of the boxes were larger than the ones he had drilled. That looked suspicious – as if some creature had somehow bored them out to increase their circumference. Without giving it much thought, he decided to swap that box's cover for the one he had just built. He made the switch as quickly as he could. He was about to leave to get ready for the next day's work when he felt an insect bite him behind the ear. Instinctively, he killed it with the back of his hand.*

Thomas stopped breathing, as if punched in the gut. Émeril noticed and stiffened. Endeavouring to speak in the most neutral tone possible, Thomas told him to finish his story and went to get his notebook to write down everything he had heard. Émeril went on.

**23:30.** *The first symptoms appeared. Émeril started to feel dizzy, with an intense headache. He had waves of hot flashes, and difficulty unclenching his jaw and relaxing his muscles. Contracting his muscles was laborious, painful. He took refuge in his room to try to sleep, but around 02:00 the symptoms intensified. He went to get help.*

Émeril stopped talking. Thomas immediately got up to auscultate him. He observed that Émeril's pulse was racing, his breathing fast, his muscles taut, his jaw clenched. The nerves on his neck seemed pulled tight enough to snap. He was feverish. Behind his ear Thomas felt the insect bite, a sensation familiar from the countless times he himself had been bitten since coming to the island. A rash was present, with swelling that emphasized the wound from the bite.

Thomas asked Émeril exactly which box's cover he had changed. Émeril showed him one marked with a recent date: one of the habitats where new horseflies had hatched the day before. These flies had yet to be injected with any virus. Thomas didn't understand. He recorded everything in his notebook, forcing himself to appear calmer than he felt. That was when Major Walker burst into the lab, alerted by soldiers who had seen a light on. The Major observed them in irate silence for a few seconds, then demanded an explanation. Thomas clearly should have left the laboratory immediately and let Major Walker resolve the situation, but he didn't want to abandon Émeril. There was no escape, not in wartime. You just had to face down whatever came your way.

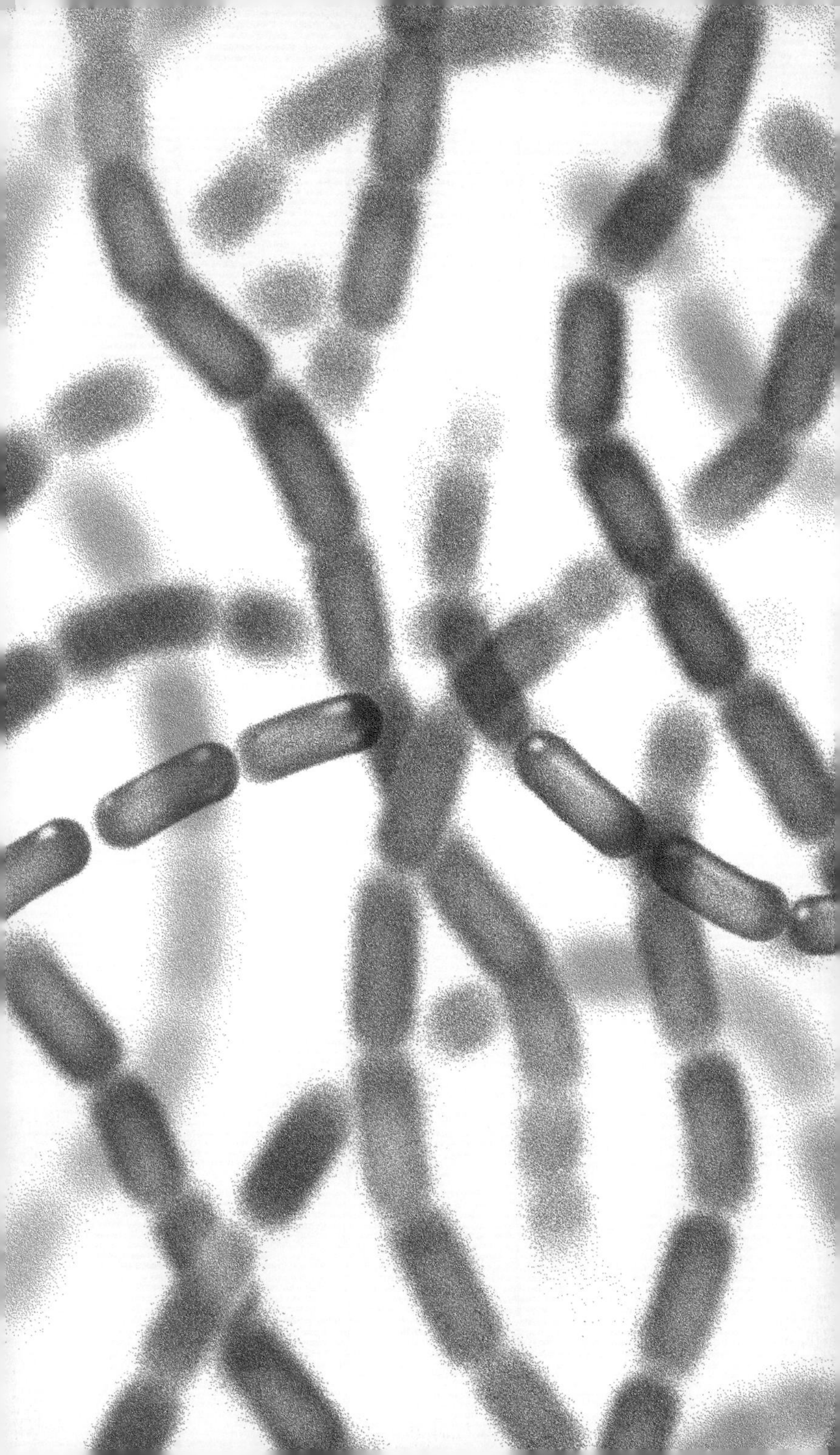

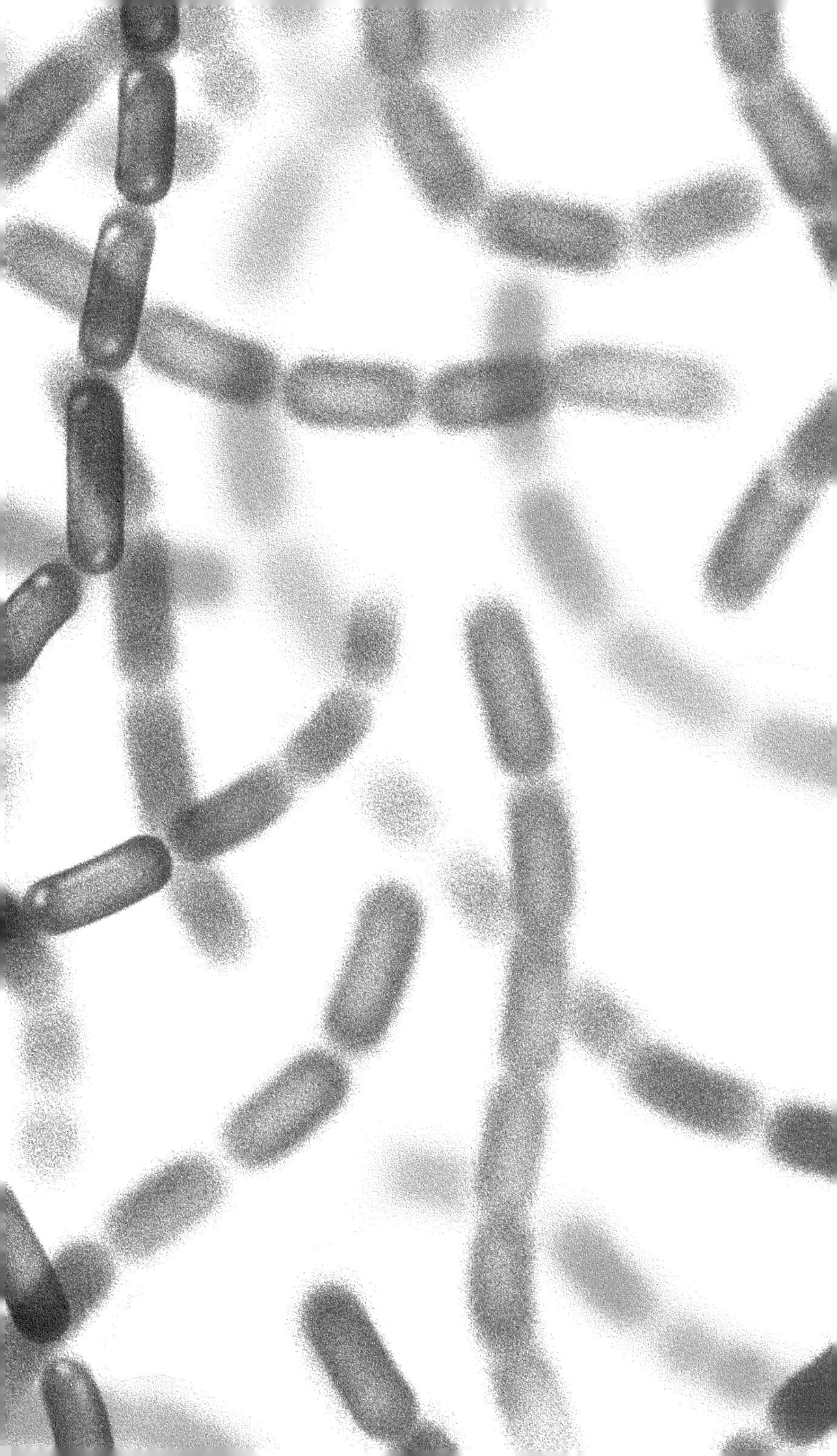

# PREY

I followed you home. Oh, if only you could have seen the state I was in. I circled you as you made your way from the factory, so closely I worried you'd notice me. Reflexively, you flailed your arms around your head, brushing my wings. I felt a swell of air uplift me, as I escaped by a whisker. The instant you opened the car door, I rushed to slip inside, landing on the rear ledge out of your sight. With my feet on the rubber, I stayed still for the length of the ride.

If there is one fear all flies share, it is dismemberment by human hands. Sometimes you are so scared of failing to kill us with your initial blow that, after knocking us out, you hold your hand in place without easing the pressure, then slide gradually back toward yourself in a drawn-out motion that can smear us onto a surface. By then you are stretching our bodies, severing our wings and our feet, which remain stuck where they first touched down. So I hid against the mat for the entire trip, too afraid to abandon myself to the thrum of the machine. Your smell was a natural aphrodisiac, with notes of sweat and metal that reminded me of blood. Even from a distance, my senses were whetted, heightened, engorged.

I can't say why I didn't go inside your home on that first day. Deep down I knew I couldn't supress my desire for long. Yet at the same time, this waiting filled every cell in my body with a delicious preorgasmic rapture. I had learned from my ancestors that patience must be cultivated; this is the very essence of the hunt.

So for a time I watched you from afar. From outside, posed on the screen of your bedroom window, I tirelessly waited each evening for you to come home from work and remove your clothes, one item at a time. You rarely stripped down completely. Sometimes, I followed you to the factory, where I spent the day observing you from above. I understood that I must not go with you on your visits to your forefather; the smell of disinfectants could not be any more repellent. At other times, when you were away, I made furtive incursions into your residence through a tiny hole I had carefully bored in the screen. What is more, I was not alone. Your apartment was abuzz with other insects and horseflies that I tried to chase away so as to keep you to myself. Once the intruders dispersed to various rooms, I surveyed your bedchamber. I smelled your clothes. I lay down on your pillow, on your bed, foraging for small flakes of dead skin, savouring each one.

In just a few days, I came to know so much about you. Your name is Theodore – this I learned from the machine triggered to speak in your absence – and you work in a factory. You don't wash every day, which I guess helps explain your olfactory charisma. You eat generous portions of meat, which may be what thickens and sweetens your blood. You are often anxious, which makes you ingest peculiar liquids to dull your reflexes before sleep. I made myself a promise: I would bite you at the earliest opportunity. Relaxed. Naked. A titch unclean. Succulent. Your dulled senses will give me time to make the incision, to dig in and search around, pierce your flesh and bore deep down, all at my leisure.

# MERCURY IN RETROGRADE

Theodore wakes in a sweat. Someone or something is about to attack. Comb as he might through his memory, he can't summon back the nightmare that haunted him, just random sensations. He recalls a menacing shadow hanging over his head, making him nervous and irritable. It kept circling back, anticipating his every move. He tries to take deep breaths, slow his heartbeat. But it feels as if his trachea has shrivelled. The oxygen takes a preposterous length of time to reach his lungs. His head hurts. He's hot, thirsty. His many bug bites have covered him in a burning itch. Blood clots on his skin show where he killed them in his sleep.

As he lies on the bed with sheets askew, Theodore's mind is racing to untangle true from false, to remember what happened the night before. Marguerite. Yet she isn't here now, next to him. Did she slip away in the night? Did she not stay at all? Had he imagined everything? No. He knows all too well that he spent the night with someone. The telltale sweet metallic smell of sex on his skin confirms his intuition. This unreal night whose contours he has been trying to trace was by a mile the most momentous event of recent years. Her. That skin, even silkier than he had imagined. There was no beginning to it, no end; his fingers could have run over her body for centuries on end without finding commencement or conclusion. There had been a tattoo of a hare, a splash of colour on her lower back.

He holds his breath, the better to catch any hint of a sound that might betray Marguerite's presence in the apartment. All he can hear is the unpleasant sounds of the horseflies against the window, searching for a way out. How was it possible that they couldn't just find the same way they'd come in? Theodore lifts himself up on his elbows to examine his surroundings, maybe even find some piece of unfamiliar clothing on the floor. The hole in the bug screen, he notices, has gotten bigger since the day before. His open lips register astonishment. He cannot clearly picture any creature capable of doing this. Right when he least expects it – *thwock* – a fly bursts in between his lips, hits the roof of his mouth, and then flies out again. His stomach turns and he coughs, scraping out his throat. How often, he wonders, do horseflies defecate?

As he ponders this question, Marguerite opens the bathroom door, sending horseflies skittering in every direction. She walks over to Theodore and, as if it were the most natural thing in the world, kisses him on the lips. He instantly freezes. He has no idea how to respond. Gone is the euphoria that gripped him yesterday, empty the store of words in his head. A single glance from Marguerite numbs him like an anaesthetic. Nothing more of worth will come. He can feel it. He knows it. Too many worries are swirling around in his head.

'It's way too hot in here!'

*What could she possibly see in him?*

'Feel like going out for breakfast, Theo?'

*He has no education.*

'Or we can stay here, if you want.'

*He barely has any money.*

'We could order something?'

*He never knows what to say.*

'How long have you lived here?'

*He swears all the time.*

'How's the soundproofing?'

*He doesn't understand fine food.*

'How far are you from the factory?'

*He could never take her to meet his parents.*

'Do you walk it sometimes?'

*Because they're dead.*

'Want to go out for a beer? After work?'

*He couldn't introduce her to his grandfather either.*

'Or a movie, maybe?'

*He doesn't really have any friends.*

'I heard they even have midnight showings now.'

*He is nothing.*

'Are you working a double today?'

*No better than nothing.*

'Call me, Theo. If you want. You can give me your number. I don't think you have a cell?'

*He is nothing.*

While Theodore tries to excavate his voice from the bottom of some ravine, Marguerite looks him up and down. She is sounding his depths, but the signal isn't getting through. Some silences speak louder than words. She gets dressed in a hurry, embarrassed that she let herself hope for more from him. On her way out, before shutting the door, she leaves him with a final thought:

'You should put up some flytraps. It's unbearable in here!'

Theodore is left alone with the horseflies, who are back up in the air, whirling like dervishes. Furious with himself for his inability to answer Marguerite, he turns on the TV, but his thoughts are painful to him. A silent grumbling in his stomach has started up again, a famished monster. He watches a New Agey–looking woman explaining the astrology behind the excess of collective rage that has taken hold in the region of Montmagny.

> Mercury is in retrograde ... full moon ... apocalyptic signs ... evil spirits ...

Theodore flips to a channel showing music videos and lets himself be hypnotized by its lurid images, intercut with the ones from the previous night replaying in his head. He is nervous, as if someone were watching him. He feels as though the flies are tracking him, their sticky dirty feet poised to land on his tongue and in his ears and nostrils. Then the shame hits him again, harder this time, like an elastic snapping back too fast and slapping his fingers. He hates this feeling. It always transports him back into his childhood memories, amplifying the pain, making him vulnerable.

He thinks back to his parents' funeral. He had just turned seven. Odd that he can summon no earlier memory. Everything before that is a gaping black hole.

The church was packed. This tragic death had awoken a sadness dormant in each person assembled, provided an outlet for each individual sorrow. People looked at Theodore and gravely nodded their heads, but no one approached to comfort him. When he was about to give his eulogy, the words would not come out. They stayed lodged deep in his chest. His grandfather gave him a signal – *start talking* – but Theodore couldn't do it. Without so much as a sorry, he rushed down the pulpit stairs and back to his seat. His eyes were as dry as his throat. Everyone stared at him. His grandfather put his hand on his shoulder and stood up to speak. His eulogy was brief, but in his humble way he honoured the memory of his son and daughter-in-law.

Theodore snaps back to reality, thinking of his grandfather, who must now be strapped to his bed. *Quick, get me out of here!* Theodore's grandfather's words spring into his mind and echo around. Without giving it further thought, he hastily gets dressed, fills a water bottle and throws it in a backpack with some grocery-store sandwiches, grabs his car keys, and sets off toward his grandfather's residence.

'Back already, Theo?' says the attendant, in a tone that conveys her displeasure to see him.

'I forgot something important.'

'We didn't know you were coming back. We had to tie up your grandfather. He's been violent today. Did you forget something?'

'My grandfather.'

'What?'

'I forgot my grandfather,' he mumbles between his teeth.

'What?'

Theodore doesn't bother repeating himself: a rage bubbles up. He climbs the stairs as fast as he can.

When he reaches the door, he goes in without knocking. His grandfather is on the bed, staring at the ceiling. Two thin chalky furrows trace the paths of the tears that have dried on his cheeks. Theodore walks over and unties the old man.

'I've come to pick you up, Émeril. C'mon. We're getting out of here.'

Theodore dresses his grandfather in clothes and a hat he finds in an old travel bag, grabs a wheelchair from the hallway, sits him down, and pushes him to the elevator. Once they hit the main floor, they find themselves face-to-face with the attendant. She glares in disapproval.

'You can't take him out for a walk. He'll get too tired in this heat wave. It's dangerous out there, with everything going on right now ...'

'We're just going for a walk.'

'He'll be unmanageable after. *No!* You can't take him out! It's not allowed!'

The attendant has raised her voice. Her face is red. She slams her fist down on the desk. Theodore is taken aback by her words, which only make him more determined. He pushes the wheelchair toward the exit, faster than before. The automatic doors slide open for the two men. A wave of hot air blankets their faces. Émeril has a coughing fit. Suddenly, Theodore hesitates. He feels stupid. He hadn't thought through the repercussions or planned where he might take his grandfather. His apartment is far too small and stuffy. A hotel room is too expensive, he doesn't have much in the bank. He is desperately casting around for a solution when Émeril breaks the silence.

'Take me to the Berthier docks. They're waiting for us at Grosse Île.'

# CAUGHT

*January 3, 1943*

A crisis cell was immediately formed at the lab and a telegram sent to inform Washington of the incident. Major Walker quarantined Émeril in one of the four rooms on the second floor, and named Thomas his official interpreter. With this role came the heavy responsibility of informing Émeril's family. Before he had even set foot on their property, he could sense Émeril's brothers staring from the porch. They went inside to get their father. Few words were exchanged. *Special mission. Lab work. Twenty-four hours a day. Duration unknown.*

Thomas could tell not one family member believed him. Seeming to sniff out his lie, the patriarch had merely squinted at Thomas and then waved him away with a look of suspicion. It felt almost like he'd aimed a weapon at Thomas and was making ready to fire. Thomas turned his back, short of breath. The cold had tightened its grasp. Could Émeril's father feel his son's despair, even over such a great distance?

Émeril was a sorry sight, a terrified bundle of confused nerves. Worse still for him than the sickness was being confined in such close quarters. Major Walker had chosen the room because its window overlooked the backwoods, out of sight of anyone walking by the base. Inside was a bed, a chamber pot, a light, and a Bible. Émeril had always lived his life outside. To make him endure solitary confinement of this kind was unconscionable. In the thrall of a terrible rage, he reverted to being a creature of raw instinct – violent, hard to approach. In the first hours of his confinement, when Thomas brought him his meal, he threw the tray against the wall and tried to escape. The soldiers had to forcibly restrain him.

No matter how many times Thomas explained that it was a temporary measure, just long enough to assess whether he was contagious, Émeril turned a deaf ear. Instead of words, muted groans issued forth from his throat, and a strange yellow gleam clouded his eyes. He foamed at the mouth when he yelled. It was as if Émeril had been swallowed by a wild beast. Though Thomas tried his best, again and again, nothing could calm the young man down. The only thing left to do was leave him alone until his anger subsided. Thomas knew this wasn't what Émeril was normally like. The horsefly bite had altered his personality. The redness in the region of the bite had spread, the swelling was even more apparent.

*January 4–6, 1943*

The next day, research in the lab resumed with even greater intensity. In the hope of finding a remedy, the scientists were working eighteen-hour days and more, going back to the hotel very late, and just to sleep. Rachelle now had to bring their meals to the lab. Since learning of Émeril's unexplained absence from his brothers, she'd stopped speaking to Thomas, not even making eye contact. This new attitude pained him.

Because his symptoms resembled those of rabies, the head virologist had given Émeril a potent dose of anti-rabies vaccine in the hope of preventing paralysis or, worse, death. He was kept under close observation, the slightest changes in his state recorded and analyzed.

Thomas was still in charge of insect research. He began by taking samples from the *Tabanus flos cadaver* species in the cage that had held the escapee. Neither he nor any of the other scientists could find the slightest trace of the virus. Was it simply too small to see with their equipment? No one could confirm it. Thomas tried another method. He carefully observed every fly in the laboratory, and took detailed notes. He was hoping to find some behavioural change, some anatomical deformity, some change of colour or other outward manifestation that might be taken as a sign of illness. He found nothing of note; they were physically identical. Next, he tried to figure out whether some of the horseflies might be contaminated. He attempted to infect a healthy individual by introducing a skin sample from a cutaneous biopsy performed on one of the specimens from the vivarium with the defective cover. He then compared their tissues under his microscope, in search of morphological or cellular anomalies that might suggest viral infection. Again, nothing.

***Observations:*** *Could the Tabanus flos cadaver have already been a carrier? If so, was it a known or an indigenous virus? Since the symptoms resemble rabies, might an anti-rabies vaccine be effective in this case?*

***Émeril's condition:*** *Pain and muscle spasms. Fever. High pulse rate and blood pressure. Confusion. Irritability. Agitation. Anxiety. Awaiting results of blood tests and first dose of anti-rabies medicine.*

*January 7–14, 1943*

With the help of the other scientists, Thomas conducted a series of experiments on rats. He placed three in a glass cage, and then introduced one of the horseflies. Once all the rats were bitten, Thomas removed the fly and isolated each specimen in a separate cage for observation. Samples were taken from each of the rats and their behaviours analyzed, but even after a week no illness was identified.

> ***Émeril's condition:*** *Fever broken. Muscle aches, particularly in neck, persistent. Heart rate and blood pressure slightly below average. Irritability. Blood test results: inconclusive. Virus not detectable. Inoculation with a second dose of anti-rabies vaccine.*

*January 15–22, 1943*

Major Walker demanded that similar tests be performed on rhesus monkeys, a species chosen for its proximity and anatomical similarity to humans. Three monkeys were transferred to a large glass cage. Thomas liberated a dozen horseflies. As soon as they were introduced, they hungrily attacked the poor creatures, biting them and sucking their blood, over and over. The biting flies were more voracious with this new prey, as if their thirst for this blood were stronger. After only ten minutes, Thomas had to pull them off to spare the animals. The monkeys were separated and placed in individual cages. The scientists noted variations in the time elapsed between viral inoculation and the onset of symptoms. Monkey No. 1 exhibited symptoms after just one hour, while it took two days in the case of Monkey No. 2; No. 3 never showed symptoms.

> ***Observations:*** *The virus presents a specific tropism in monkeys, and therefore potentially in humans as well. Incubation periods vary from one individual to the next. Some did not immediately develop the illness. Impossible to confirm, however, whether they were resistant, immunized, or asymptomatic carriers.*

This third possibility – *asymptomatic carriers* – filled Thomas with dread. He had himself been bitten by the *Tabanus flos cadaver* countless times over the course of the summer. Could he be an unwitting carrier? Would he develop the disease one day? Was he contagious? He knew all too well that he should have informed his colleagues, starting with Major Walker, but couldn't bring himself to do it. He knew that his life was at risk. He pushed on in the laboratory, working twice as hard.

> ***Émeril's state:*** *Noticeable relaxation of muscles. Pulse and blood pressure normalized. Irritable. Third inoculation with anti-rabies vaccine.*

*January 23–February 2, 1943*

Around twenty monkeys were now infected. A trend had emerged: 25 per cent of individuals presented no clear sign of the disease. In the others, symptoms always appeared in the same order but with varying degrees of severity – high in certain individuals, like Émeril. There was always significant swelling and itching in the vicinity of the bite, followed by muscle spasms or tremors in affected body parts. In more severe cases, hydrophobia manifested within hours of infection, followed by fever, spasms, and acute agitation. Only 20 per cent of infected specimens appeared to present hallucinations, convulsions, or persistent anger.

> ***Observations:*** *The nervous system seems to be irredeemably affected in 20 per cent of contaminated specimens. While repeated inoculation with anti-rabies vaccines seems to stimulate the autoimmune system and produce an acceptable response to the virus, some individuals seem to never completely recover.*

> ***Émeril's state:*** *Stable. Persistent irritability. Inoculation with a final dose of anti-rabies vaccine.*

*February 3–14, 1943*

After a telegram from Washington, Major Walker asked the researchers to place an infected monkey in cohabitation with an uninfected one. They obeyed. As soon as the two animals found themselves in the same enclosed space, a relationship of domination was established. The monkey that had been bitten by horseflies dominated the one that had not by adopting intimidating body language, stealing its meals, and dumping out its water bowl. The monkeys were then separated and placed under observation. In the following days, when a non-infected monkey was bitten by the contaminated monkey, it did not develop the disease. The outcome was the same each time they repeated the experiment.

> ***Hyphothesis:*** *The virus is propagated exclusively by the bite of the Tabanus flos cadaver and not by a contaminated individual.*

> ***Émeril's State:*** *Stable with spontaneous and uncontrollable fits of rage. Not contagious.*

*February 15–March 1, 1943*

Unsatisfied with the results of the last experiment, Major Walker ordered that the four monkeys presenting the most severe symptoms be locked up together, to observe their behaviour in a group setting. In less than five minutes it was clear that they could not be left together in an enclosed space without the risk of seeing them fight each other to the death.

The largest rhesus monkey immediately attacked the weakest one, charging, clawing, biting, and slapping it. Aided by soldiers, the scientists had to use rifle butts to separate the animals. Thomas watched the scene unfold from outside the cage, at Major Walker's side. The Major's eyes were shining and a satisfied smile crept over his face. He hurried off to send another telegram to Washington.

*March 2, 1943*

The orders came in almost immediately: Thomas was assigned to accompany Émeril to a laboratory close to Washington, where he would undergo further testing. Thomas thought immediately of his own father, who had once told him, *You never know who your true enemies are until you place your trust in them.* How right he had been.

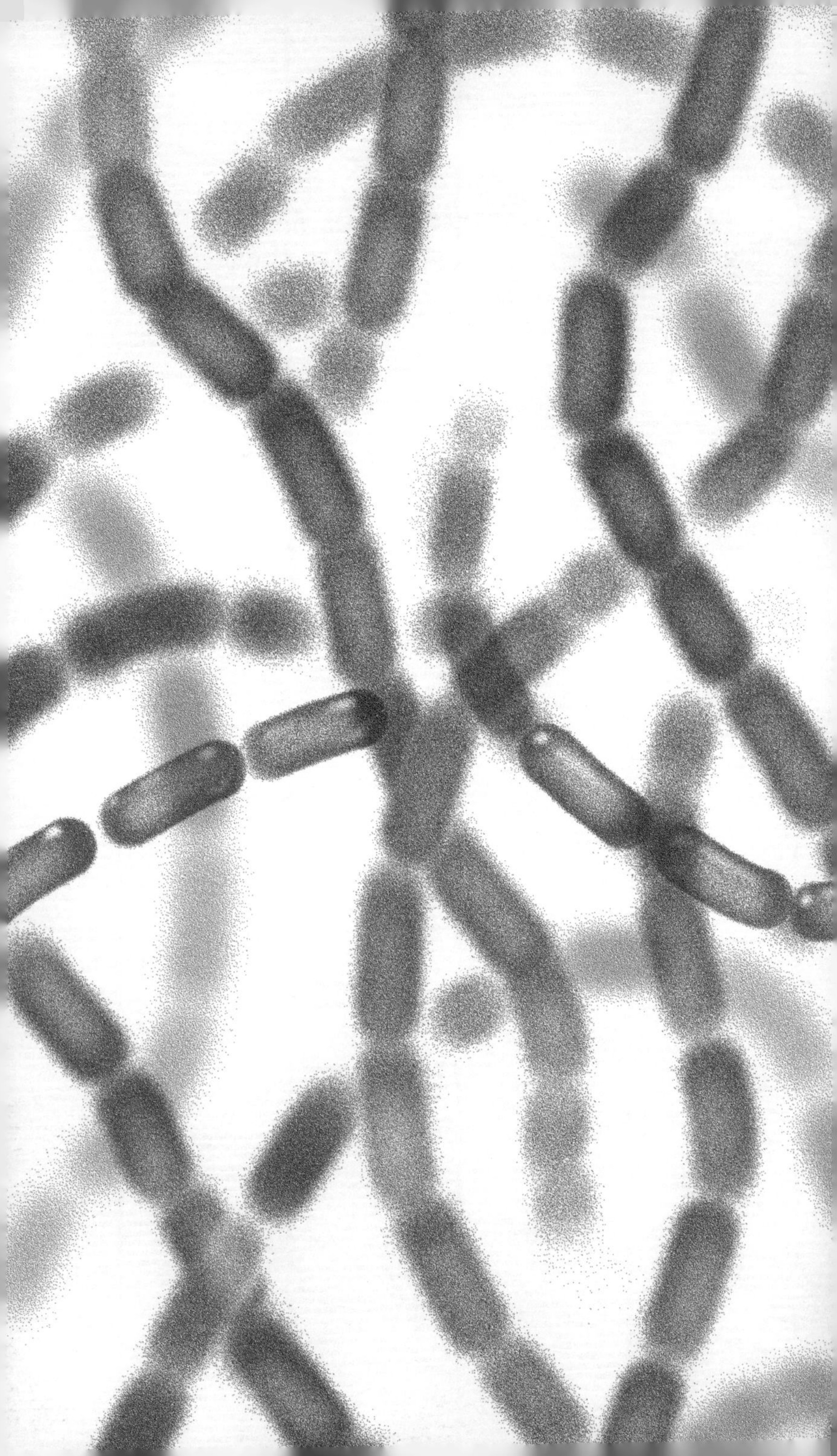

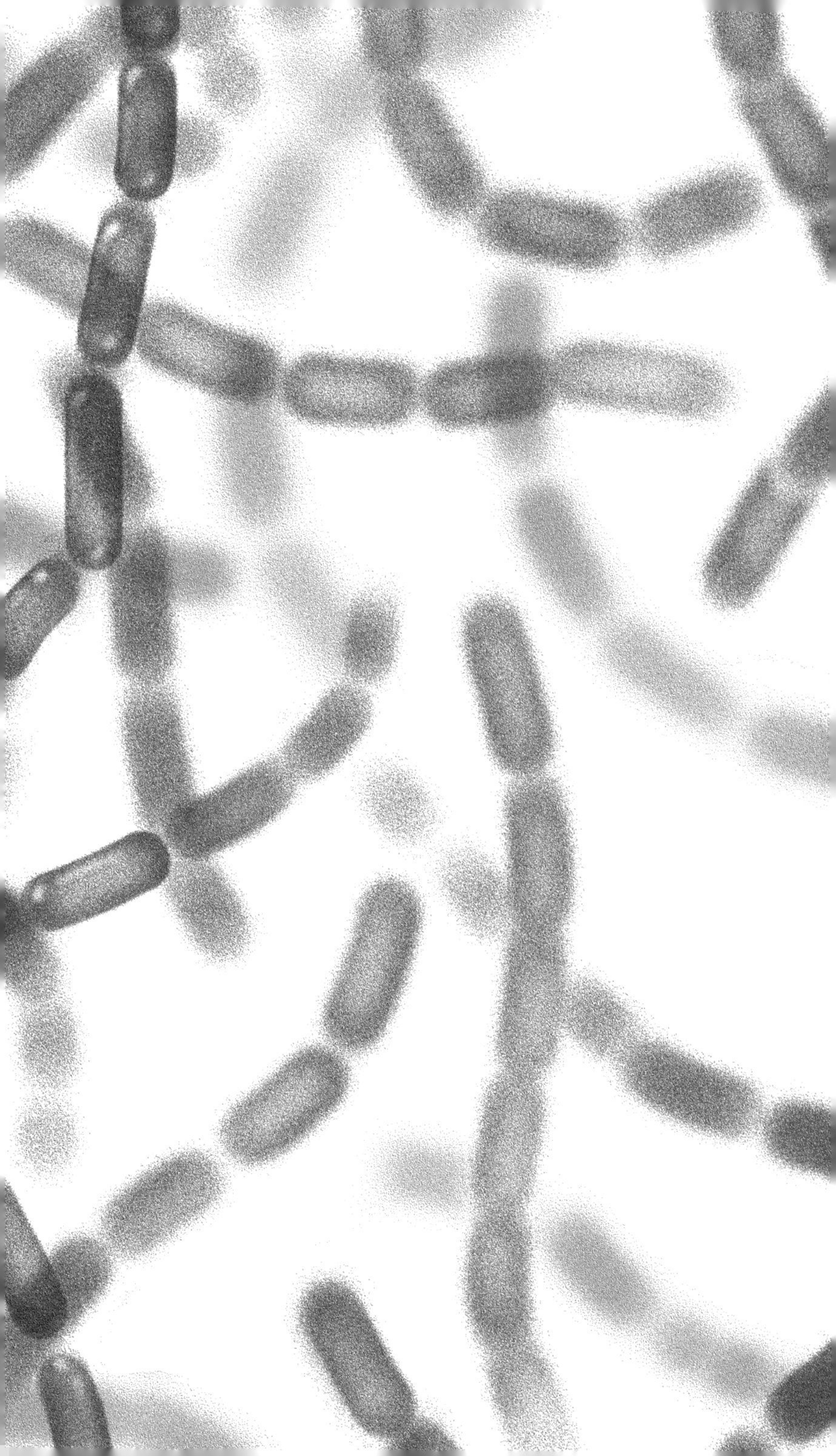

## COITUS

Unfortunately, things didn't go the way I thought they would. After two days away, you retreated into your home and sunk into mute apathy. You wolfed down your pungent meal without taking the time to chew, then nearly passed out on your bed, though the sun was still high in the sky. You would certainly have made an easy prey. Others of my kind might have swept in to take advantage, but such a course was not for me – not yet. It would not have fully satisfied my thirst for pleasure. Instead I watched you sleep, all day, in crushing heat. Hourly you tossed and turned in search of a cooler patch of bedding. And then, after nightfall, you impulsively leapt up as if your life depended on it. You took a shower, applied fragrance, got dressed, and slammed the apartment door. I didn't follow because I could not take your nauseating new smell. I stayed inside, waiting for you.

Most people know that flies don't sleep at night. When evening comes, we slow our metabolism and ease into a state of torpor called *the quiescent state*. We remain conscious of our environments and register sensory stimuli, but our reactions are far slower than in daytime. So while you were away I placed myself on standby. It took a healthy fraction of a second to gather my wits when you came back in. At first I did not realize that you weren't alone. Your behaviour was erratic. Your odour had not totally returned, even though you were sweating profusely. A second chemical scent had been added to the mix. I was instantly repulsed. Your half-naked body was entwined with the body of another of your kind. Your movements were so highly synchronized I could not distinguish you from the other one. I approached; it was crucial to observe more closely. You removed the woman's last remaining articles of clothing, took her in your arms, and lifted her up to the height of your face. Your mouth seemed poised to swallow her whole.

Desire rose up from my depths. I cracked, succumbed, gave in, let drop my final shred of self-control. Unable to restrain myself another moment, I flew around you in shrinking concentric circles. My senses were whetted by being so close to you. I danced around for a few minutes, correcting my flight path to keep it aligned with your movements. And then I took the plunge. No words can convey what I felt when I landed on you. Every neuron in my legs bristled to life, setting off powerful electrical impulses in each of my extremities. I scoured your skin in search of the perfect patch, the one that would procure a supreme bliss. I slid my tongue into the hollow of your right knee and ran it up and down your flank and over your neck. But of course my search ended in the area behind your ear. That's where the skin is softest, where we can hear the blood coursing with every beat of your heart. On the underside of your earlobe, I listened as your breathing grew louder and shorter, and I set down my spongy mouth. A sense of unbounded euphoria gripped me. I did not wait another second, and with a flick of my head I plunged my stylet into your skin. The incision immediately created a wound, sending lymph and blood flowing into me through no effort of my own. Was it on my account that you cried out in orgasm? I cannot say. But you collapsed onto the bed, our connection unsevered. I kept on drinking from you for a few more seconds longer before you noticed my presence. I felt a wave of revulsion wash over you.

With a brusque and brutal movement you unseated me, interrupting my coitus, forcing me to fly away, dizzy, my mouth full of blood. I couldn't immediately parse the emotion that stole over me then, as my survival instinct screamed loud and clear, *Flee!* Only later, as I began to digest your flesh, did I at last understand the rage inside me.

# A DIFFERENT WAY OF LOOKING

At 2 p.m. on the dot, Theodore turns right onto Rue de l'Anse, the last straight stretch of their drive to Berthier-sur-Mer. Émeril stares out the window. He is breathtakingly calm, as if what they are doing is the most normal thing in the world. Theodore notices that his grandfather appears to have suddenly become a much younger man. As their destination nears, he grows taller in his seat. His back straightens. His head looks less heavy, his eyes brighter. It reminds Theodore of his childhood, when his grandfather would take him fishing.

'Park here,' Émeril orders.

Theodore does what he's told and cuts the engine. He looks around. People are swarming all over the marina, searching for a breath of cool air that remains elusive, even this late in the day.

'Help me up.'

Theodore gets out first. Immediately, at least ten horseflies start circling him. Despite his best efforts to shoo them away with his arms, they keep coming back. He puts on his backpack and helps his grandfather get up.

'Low tide soon. If we don't get a move on we'll get caught in the channel!'

Reluctant to contradict his grandfather, Theodore does as the old man says. He also starts seriously wondering whether he should try to make him see reason. Émeril urges him to move faster, then pushes away his grandson's arm and walks off toward the marina on his own. For a man his age he's improbably fast. All around, there is no ignoring the nervous energy of the boaters. Down on the dock, three men are fighting for no apparent reason. One pushes another, who falls off the dock into the water. After the splash, their yelling echoes out. Émeril acts like he hasn't seen or heard a thing and weaves around the people effortlessly. All of a sudden, he's walking down to the aluminum floating dock. The tide is low, the incline steep; Theodore hurries to give his grandfather a hand. Together, they narrowly avoid the cluster of men, who are still arguing and have begun throwing punches. Police sirens wail in the distance.

'Grandpa, I think we should … '

'C'mon, let's take that boat there.'

'Grandpa, you know I can't drive a boat.'

'Stop your whining! Follow me!'

Before Theodore can finish his sentence, his grandfather is lifting a leg over the side of an old grey aluminum boat and taking a seat on the bench. Theodore looks around nervously. The dock fight is escalating; new people are joining in. A young marina employee tries to help the man who fell into the water by throwing him a life buoy, but then he too is pushed into the river. Unsure what to do and unable to say no to his grandfather, Theodore jumps into the boat and sits facing the old man.

'What are you waiting for? Pull in the line!'

A man with a bloody nose comes over to them. He's foaming at the mouth. *What if this is his boat?* Theodore wonders. Impatiently, Émeril stands up to untie the line, but he loses his balance; his grandson catches him just in time.

'Just like your father. Can't do nothing right!'

With wounded pride, Theodore helps Émeril sit down, impulsively pulls in the line, and pushes off from the dock with his foot, before the man can reach them. One second, two seconds, three ... The boat drifts away from the dock. There's no going back now. The unknown man facing them falls off the side of the dock, convulsing. Should Theodore go back and help? What is he doing? He watches his grandfather, who doesn't seem to even see what is going on around him.

'Now lower the motor into the water.'

Theodore is paralyzed by this situation that shows no signs of improving. At the dock, the police have arrived. The water is muddy and choppy, the sun blinding. While Theodore gets ready to yell something, his grandfather grabs his face in one hand and stares deep into Theodore's eyes.

'Listen to me, boy. This might be my last trip. So do what I say. Put the motor in the water.'

Theodore remembers the sight of his grandfather tied to his bed. He takes a deep breath. 'How?'

'Pull that lever there and she'll go down.'

Theodore does as he's told.

'Now squeeze the bulb a few times to prime her. You should feel some resistance. Stop. Stop! Now put it in neutral. Yeah, like that. Give her some choke. Right! Now pull the ripcord.'

The motor fails to start on the first pull.

'Put some arm into it. Harder, dammit!'

When the motor finally starts, Theodore yells with joy. Émeril smiles at him and gives him encouraging taps on the shoulder.

'What do you know, we might make a man of you after all. Now let 'er rip! Let's go.'

Theodore turns the tiller handle to give the motor more gas and accelerates, steering toward the centre of the channel so he doesn't bottom out.

'Gonna be tight.'

Theodore keeps a firm hold on the tiller as they make their way through the passage. He manoeuvres around the breakwater and finds himself out in the St. Lawrence River proper. The open water is grey as far as the eye can see, and a smudgy finger of fog is brushed over the horizon line. Theodore remembers the one time the old man took him out fishing on the river. A few years had passed since his parents' death. The wind that day was fairly strong, the water rough and covered with fleecy patches of foam. Theodore didn't yet know that you could avoid seasickness by not looking at the water. He tried to conceal his sickly pallor and slow movements. His disappointed, irritated grandfather made them turn back before they caught a single fish. He'd never taken Theodore out fishing on a boat again, just let him cast off from the dock once in a while. Theodore spent that night puking his guts out.

Now Émeril starts speaking again, but his tone of voice brings back even more memories for Theodore.

'On days like today you can't tell the sky from the land. You've gotta find a different way of looking.'

Theodore watches him for a few long seconds, chewing on that last sentence. Émeril keeps talking.

'When you can't see a thing, you listen. Smell.'

He signals to his grandson to stop talking.

'The gulls behind you. The echo of the other boats. Hear it? The rush of the wind? The waves. The currents pulling us one way or another. The direction of the clouds, those high ones. And the ones lower down too. The ebb, the swell. Berthier's got the biggest tides on the St. Lawrence. Seven metres! Hear that? Drown a man before you can blink.'

Carefully, Émeril stands up, takes a deep breath of air as he squints, and licks a finger to suss out the direction of the wind. He waits a few seconds and then sits again.

'Point her west. Let's see if you can steer this thing! The tide's dropping fast. Currents down there could take us right by the island, if we don't watch it. Don't ever trust those currents! They've sent plenty of good men to the bottom.'

'But how can we get to Grosse Île?'

'Oh, don't worry about that. I could get there with my eyes closed.'

Theodore, who has no idea which way is west, steers the boat in the direction his grandfather pointed and cranks the gas, full speed ahead. The bow jumps up and slaps down onto the waves. Émeril almost falls overboard.

'Not so fast, boy! You don't want to bottom out the motor. Last thing we need is an accident.'

Theodore slows down a bit, and looks at his grandfather. The old man seems thirty years younger. Behind him, the town has almost receded from view on the horizon. Theodore breathes deep into his lungs to ease his anxiety and checks the time. He should be at work, should have been there at least fifteen minutes ago, but it's as if he has lost the ability to care. The boat cuts through the water, leaving behind a wake that immediately vanishes. His grandfather is perched on the bow, looking straight ahead. Theodore feels a bewildering calm as the boat chugs forward at a steady pace. The wind sweeping his face gives him an airy sense of freedom.

After about an hour and a few redirections from Émeril, Theodore sees a single brown line on the water, followed by several smaller ones. Then, wide buildings of indeterminate colour emerge from the ground, like grey ghosts on rocky shores. He feels his heart skip a beat as what they are doing sinks in. How did he get himself into this mess?

'There's Grosse Île,' says Émeril, pointing an index finger forward. 'To the right, that's Île la Sottise and Île Sainte Marguerite. We'll land on the eastern shore, so no one sees us. There's still tourists around, on the upper dock, but they'll be leaving soon. We'll drop anchor in the bay for now.'

'What are we gonna do on the island, Grandpa?'

'I've got to pick something up. Something important.'

# THE MISSION

*March 3–9, 1943*

When Thomas told him about the mission, Émeril was apprehensive. But he came around before long; he would have done anything to get out of that room. Eight weeks, fifty-nine days, one thousand four hundred and sixteen hours of captivity had been an irredeemable torture. Hibernation had blunted his senses. He could now better contain his flights of rage, but still could not fully control them. When the fits struck, isolation was the best remedy; after a few hours he would calm down again.

Major Walker had been pressuring them to leave as soon as possible, but winter refused to co-operate. Even with March upon them, the great river remained inscrutable, unnavigable. From whatever vantage point they chose, the St. Lawrence resembled a battlefield, with columns of icicles pointing upward as if waiting to impale them. A thick fog hung like a broad curtain of smoke where the horizon met the waterline. The wind blew without reprieve. Fine powdery snow had covered everything, rising in banks so high around the lab and the hotel that they struggled to get around them. Every day at dawn, guarded by a soldier, Thomas took Émeril out of his room. Together they walked along the shoreline, striving to keep a low profile. Émeril studied the river and the horizon, the ice and the echo. His verdict was immediate: high winds, strong currents, poor visibility, rising tide. Thomas always left him more time than strictly necessary. These few minutes outside were vital for Émeril, as if they were bringing him back to life, right down deep in his guts.

*March 10, 1943*

08:45. Openings in the river's ice cover were the first sign of spring. The drifting floes in the middle of the river also seemed to have stopped moving, as if the wind had eased up at last. Émeril gave the green light for a departure. He'd have to get the winter canoe ready, prep all the gear, and gather his brothers for the crossing. It was Thomas's job to fetch them. They greeted him with a suspicion that he had no words to allay. He mumbled some confused explanation. As they made their way back, Thomas opted for silence. When Émeril's father and brothers saw their lost family member standing beside the canoe, they looked each other over, at length and in turn. Then a polite smile crept over everyone's faces, and they tapped Émeril on the shoulder. Thomas sensed their animosity and stared at the ground. No one asked about Émeril's prolonged absence or his work in the lab; above all, no one mentioned the state he was in. It was impossible to ignore the suffering on Émeril's face. He appeared several years older. Émeril shot his family a quick look, and Thomas had the distinct feeling that they understood each other perfectly without saying a word.

Once preparations for the journey were complete, Major Walker, Émeril's father, Thomas, the crew, and the soldier found themselves on the shore, patiently waiting for the tide to ebb and the ice to set off on its slow drift east. Émeril showed Thomas where to sit in the middle of the ice canoe, after tying down the sealed drum that would sit between Thomas's legs. It held fifty horseflies in beakers and the frozen bodies of four euthanized macaques. The soldier sat behind Thomas, looking even more terrified than the young scientist was. Émeril and his brothers took seats on either side of the oak canoe, which seemed to weigh a ton, and started shoving it and running alongside it, with one leg in the canoe and the other pushing against the shifting pans of ice. The surface creaked and cracked as they made their way forward. They left behind Émeril's father and Major Walker, two men receding wordlessly into the distance like a wall of snow.

10:20. From the start, the crossing felt like chaos. Within minutes, the ice canoeists realized there was no open water ahead, just moving ice floes. As the men pushed the canoe forward, the sheets crashed up against each other, splitting and lifting to ride over each other with deafening shrieks that joined the roar of the wind. Émeril and his brothers had to get in and out of the canoe at every obstacle in the ice, to keep pulling, pushing, and hauling. Sometimes the ice piled into heaps close to two metres high, taller than them. It was a herculean labour. After his weeks in solitary confinement, it left Émeril panting. The two passengers did their best to stay in their places in the canoe. Sensing that he would soon be seasick, Thomas stared out at a small point in the middle of the gleaming white ice, but before long it left his field of vision. The wind swelled, the sky cast over in clouds darker than even Émeril and his brothers could have anticipated. A solid curtain of snow began to fall. After just an hour, they couldn't see more than five paces in front of them. Fierce headwinds started blowing, catching the entire group by surprise and pulling them into a current they could never haul themselves out of. Though they battled hard for a solid hour, straining to cover the half kilometre to a break in the ice cover where they could put their boat in water again, it was in vain.

Thomas was petrified. At first he didn't fully understand why the men sat down, resigned and exhausted, after pulling the ice canoe up onto a large bench of ice. They exchanged a few looks, a wordless debate on the subject of survival. Each took a sip of water. Carefully, Thomas asked Émeril what was happening. Émeril made it clear: there was nothing to be done.

'We have to wait for the storm to blow over. That's just the way it is. It's not our first time. There's no fighting nature.'

After a short rest, Émeril and his brothers got back to work under the inquisitive stares of Thomas and the soldier. With an ease that made it look like they had done each step a thousand times before, they took a tarp from the back of the canoe and stretched it above their heads, held up with an oar placed upright like a mast. The corners of the sail were lashed to the canoe. Émeril poured some oil into an old bucket he set down at his feet and lit a fire. Curls of black smoke swirled around them. Thomas felt suddenly as if he were asphyxiating, but one of Émeril's brothers pulled out his knife and cut a hole in the tarp at its highest point to let the smoke escape. Then he sat back down and covered his face with his coat.

'Now, we wait.'

The soldier didn't understand French. Thomas repeated what he had just heard, and the soldier stared back so dumbfounded that Thomas preferred to look away. Then the storm took possession of their bodies, and no one dared breathe another word. At times the wind kicked up and blew so hard inside their shelter that the men felt certain they would be sucked up into the heavens at any moment; at other times a lull descended and they could even hear the ice chunks creaking, interlocking and smashing into each other, like gaping jaws opening up to crush them. An hour passed, and then another, and a third and a fourth and a fifth, and the wind kept on howling. Despite their makeshift cabin and the fire they lit for a few minutes every half-hour, every man was shivering from head to toe, facing down the creep of hypothermia. The soldier hadn't moved for so long Thomas figured he had turned into a block of ice on his bench. Émeril regularly popped his head outside the tarp to look off into the distance. Then he exchanged a look with his brothers, who seemed to understand. Thomas said nothing at all.

15:25. The sound of the river changed, almost imperceptibly. A stillness descended, the wind subsided. Émeril noticed first. The tide was at its midpoint. Émeril began moving around, and his brothers sprang into action too. They lifted up the tarp, folded it, and stared at the shore for a few minutes. Half-frozen and exhausted, they still managed to dislodge the canoe and start pushing again. Thomas held on even tighter to his barrel, wondering where they had found the strength to push on. After a while they took another break, to talk. They stared off in the distance and pointed at a precise point on the horizon that Thomas could not identify. They got trekking again, pushing the canoe. A few long minutes later, Thomas understood what was happening. Through the slowly dissipating fog of snow, he saw a bright light flickering in the distance. Émeril and his brothers were driving them toward it. At last, the current let them make real progress. They were slowly but surely approaching the shore. As they drew nearer, Thomas saw that the light was a fire, lit by the army as a beacon to guide them. He looked over at the soldier beside him, but the man was unresponsive, staring straight ahead with open eyes and purple lips. Thomas turned around again. From then on he kept his eyes fixed on the flame.

After their exhausting battle against the river, the canoeists finally pulled the boat up onto the frozen shore and set it on a great block of ice. Almost before they had time to take a breath, soldiers swaddled them in thick boiled-wool blankets and sat them in horse-drawn sledges. They were taken immediately to the army base, where Émeril was separated from his brothers. No one protested; they were far too exhausted. Thomas was given a private room, connected to Émeril's. He spent the night trying to warm his limbs. His blood was no longer circulating, blocked somewhere in the centre of his chest. He felt as if, at some point in the crossing, his body had metamorphosed into ice; as if he himself were drifting on the pack ice. He had no idea how to get back.

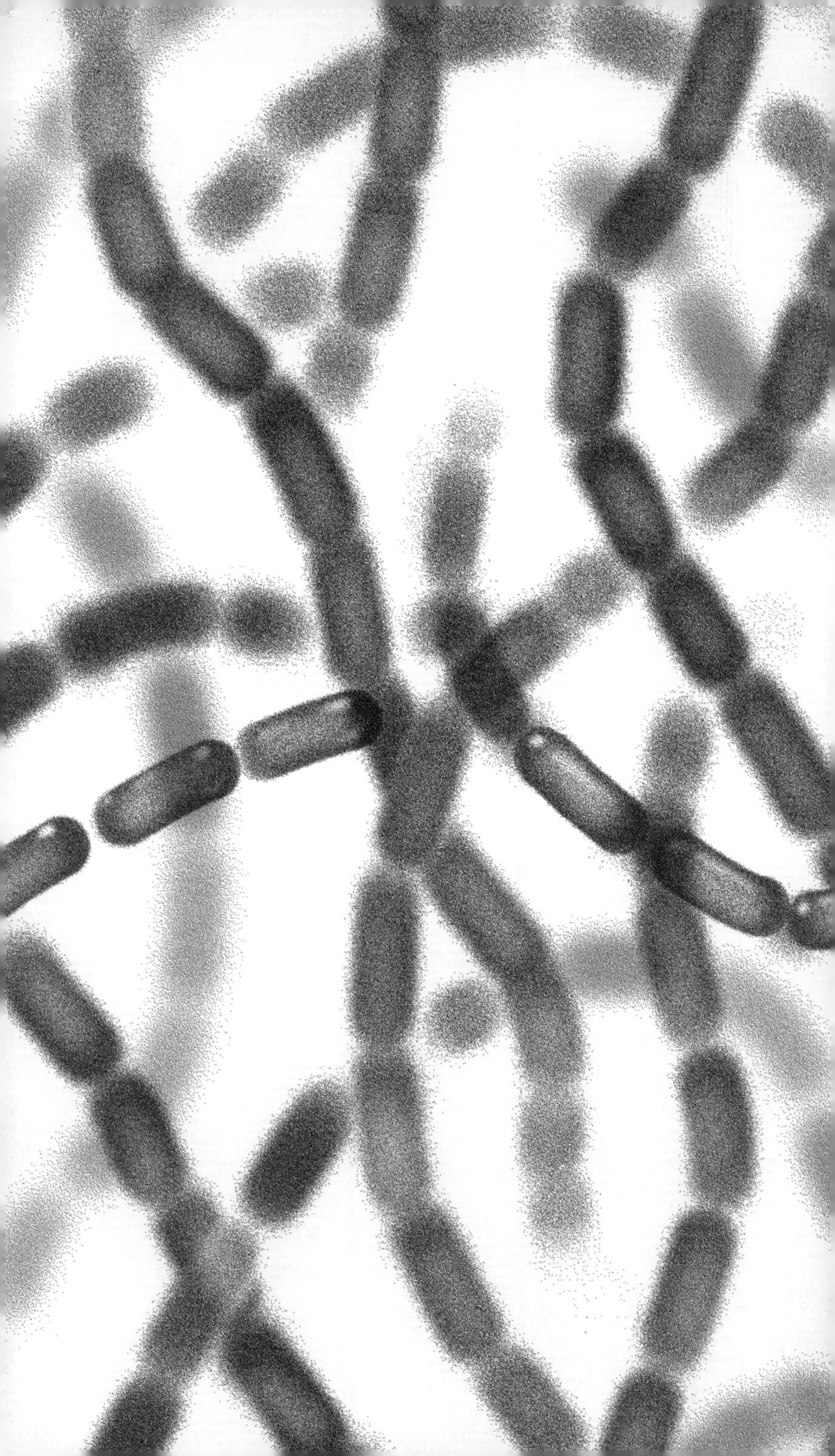

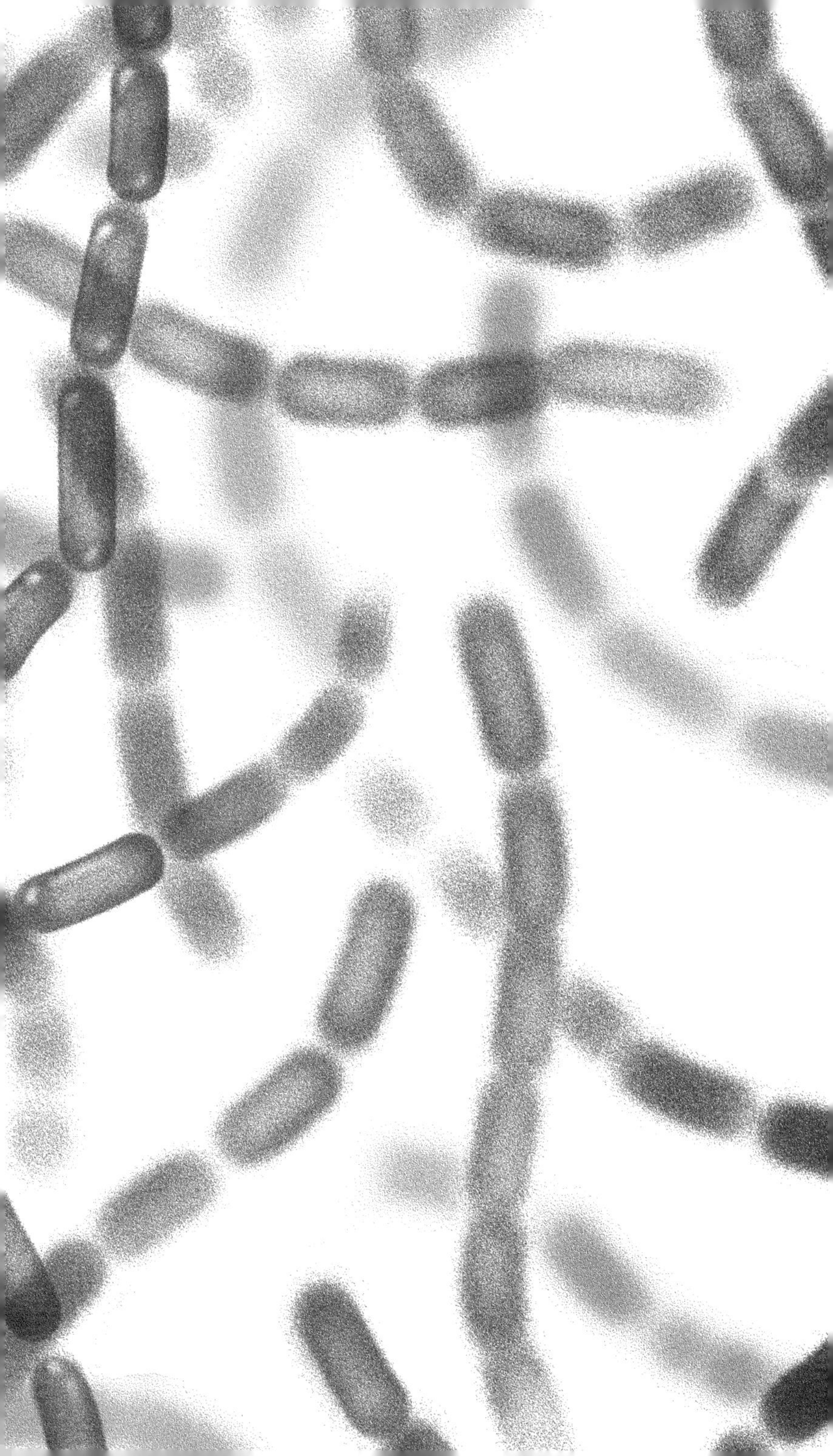

## RAGE

There are no words to convey the degree to which I was vexed, riled, bereft, annoyed, impatient, frustrated, indignant, impotent, resigned, piqued, furious, bitter, hard-hearted, hysterical, disturbed, fervid, fierce, furious, and rabid, inhabited by the destructive rage that has colonized my entire being since that fateful day. When I think of you and your species in general, and of that woman in particular, of your feeble bodies and trifling minds, a jumble of invisible strings are yanked inside me, tied in knots that thwart my peace of mind. I feel the rage sweep over me, in every cell of my body. I don't know how it could have lain so long below the surface. Admittedly, this anger has always been in me, an invasive presence deep in my genes. Now that you have revived this force, it swells exponentially whenever I am close to you, close to your kind. The heat of your bodies coming together in space amplifies my rage, makes me yearn to cause you suffering, to destroy all that you touch and all that you have laboured to build over centuries with such absurd determination. I despise you. I abhor you. I detest you. I recoil from you. Never have I seen individuals act with such malevolence toward themselves and others.

You are everywhere. You think only of yourselves. Your overpowering chemical odours spread, along with the pollution you generate. You defile everything you come across, cannot even be bothered to erase the trace of your passage. In fact, the opposite is true: destruction is your one means of expression. You're isolated from your habitat. How long since you lost the ability to read the changes to your environment, to decipher the behaviours handed down by your ancestors – the very customs that permitted you to survive up to now? At this exact moment, you must feel fear. A visceral and atavistic dread in the pit of your stomach. Are you blind and deaf to the signals our species is sending out as we make ready to attack you? We have decided to harass you, impede you, infect you. And we are surely not alone. You have so profoundly tipped the balance that there can now be no going back. You will be removed; it's a matter of time. The Earth cannot support you much longer. I dream of the moment it expels you from its great throat, like a mouthful of rotten food. I, for one, will rejoice. We shall all be filled with joy, free at last from your presence, from your failure. No one signed a contract with you for all eternity.

## APPROACHING THE ISLAND

After steering around Île la Sottise and Île Sainte Marguerite, Émeril and Theodore circle the island and approach from the southeast, where the headland is less steep. A great heron stares at them from a distance, unfolding its wings as they pass. Theodore cuts the motor and lets the boat slowly drift, pulled in by the waves. The tide is low. Émeril warns Theodore not to get close to the shore; it's better to drop anchor several metres out.

'How will we get onto the island? Are we supposed to wait for low tide? Or high tide?'

His grandfather ignores him. Émeril stands up with care and then swings first one leg and then the other over the side of the boat. The water comes up to his thighs. With an astonishing confidence he strides through the water toward the bank, arms outstretched to keep his balance. He makes steady progress over what must be a treacherous shoal. It's as if his feet know the route of an invisible path. Theodore also gets out of the boat, much less gracefully than his grandfather. He loses his balance and almost keels over into the water, freezes in an unlikely position, and regains his balance just in time. Émeril looks back, irritated.

'Quit flapping around. You're gonna get us caught!'

Theodore's undivided attention is focused on his legs as he silently makes his way through the water, but his feet get stuck in the gloopy clay at the river bottom. His shoes make a deep squelching, as if the river were delighting in holding them tight in its mouth. Émeril greets each sound with a cluck of disapproval. Theodore makes his way forward as best he can, absorbed in this dance of restraint. He doesn't immediately see that his grandfather is already on dry land, waiting for him on a log. Now Theodore too emerges from the water, traversing the final few metres of sharp-edged rushes and slippery clay. He's soaked. His head is spinning; drops of sweat trickle down his back. A dozen horseflies are circling. For the tenth time today, Theodore wonders why he agreed to undertake this tortuous journey with his grandfather. First kidnapping, now trespassing: he may well end up in jail. Finally, Theodore sets foot on the sand and hauls his heavy body toward his grandfather. The effort has wrung every iota of strength from his body. He sits down next to the old man and tries to catch his breath.

'Approaching the island is tough. This bay is where we used to come for peace and quiet. Watch out for the poison ivy!'

Theodore tenses up. He doesn't like the idea of poison ivy, not one bit. He's not sure he could even recognize it. He has had only one run-in with the toxic plant, when he was young, but still holds vivid memories of the torment. His grandfather has read his mind, and promises to show him how to avoid it. Reassured to a point, Theodore takes the water bottle from his bag and passes it to his grandfather, who takes a swig. They pass it back and forth and share a sandwich of dubious freshness. Émeril doesn't eat his half right away. Instead, he walks around the shoreline awhile and comes back with a handful of greens.

'What's that, Grandpa?'

'Wild chives, boy. Put some in your sandwich. You won't believe how good it is!'

Theodore does what he is told and takes a bite. The sharp oniony taste lashes his tongue and tickles his nose, but he eats it in silence anyway. He doesn't want to disappoint his grandfather. He finishes his sandwich in a hurry, then washes it down with some water.

'What do we do now?'

'Wait.'

'What are we waiting for?'

Instead of answering, his grandfather lies down in the sand in the shade of a scraggly tree and pulls his hat down over his eyes. Theodore tries to do the same, but is worried that wandering tourists or some worker will see their boat anchored off the coast. When he does doze off, he drifts in and out of short nightmares spliced together from his worst childhood memories. Only when his grandfather wakes him with a gentle kick to the ribs does he realize he was fully asleep.

'Enough! Enough lying around, c'mon!' says Émeril, unfolding his clothes. 'It'll be light just long enough to cross the island and find what I came here for.'

Theodore stumbles to his feet. He had underestimated the energy needed for their crossing and the walk to shoreline. How is his grandfather still standing? Despite his old age, the man shows no sign of fatigue; his very being, his soul, seems at home here. Theodore's bulky, clumsy body wastes huge amounts of energy. He helps Émeril cross through a bush and step over some logs. Together, they come through into a long flat grassy stretch.

'See that there? It's the cemetery. There's another one, but you can't go there.'

Theodore looks around. A dozen metres in front of him, a collection of gravestones seems to have appeared out of nowhere. Their state of disrepair makes Theodore feel like he's in a horror movie. He shivers. Theodore has never liked cemeteries, has never even visited his parents' graves.

'This is where your great-grandparents are buried. Even after everything that happened, my father still wanted to be buried here. Next to my mother.'

Émeril points at two gravestones, side by side, and walks over for a moment of silent reflection. Theodore senses a furtive shadow in the corner of his eye. He turns around and scans the horizon: nothing. Inside he feels a sense of growing dread. He does not like it here. There's no doubt in his mind; they should never have come to Grosse Île.

'It wasn't just immigrants who were quarantined here,' Émeril continues. 'People don't know the whole story. C'mon, let's go left, over the bridge.'

Feeling his grandson's hesitation, Émeril shows him which way to go. They walk for a while, and their path merges with a rugged dirt road that is the island's main thoroughfare. In the distance, Theodore sees four buildings on either side of the road. As they near the first one, his grandfather stops by the front door.

'That was the hospital, for the ones with the pox. That's what they called it, when Grosse Île was a quarantine island. But we had our own name for it.'

'What do you mean, *we*?'

'They kept all kinds of little glass bottles here. Had to watch we didn't break 'em.'

Émeril turns back to the river, and Theodore follows his gaze. In front of them is Île la Sottise, like a rocky castle wall, with metres of grassy shoreline and the river between them. Their sudden stop here has again piqued the horseflies' interest.

'You smell too strong. What kind of guy goes around in perfume?' says the old man.

Émeril is edging along the bay, pulling out rushes and bringing them back to Theodore.

'Here, scrub yourself with these. Then they'll leave you alone a bit more.'

Theodore obeys. The stalks are sharp, cool to the touch. They exfoliate his skin, though the sand is an irritant. Theodore doesn't protest; he knows his grandfather will never yield an inch.

'What were you doing here, Grandpa?' Theodore asks, with a hint of concern.

'Bad things, boy. I was helping them do very bad things.'

'Like what?'

'People thought they were smarter than everyone else. Playing with life and death. If they were still alive today, they wouldn't feel good about it. They wouldn't feel good at all. They must be turning over in their graves.'

'Who?'

'There's something here. We should've let sleeping dogs lie.'

Theodore climbs up onto the front porch of an abandoned infirmary, looks into the window built into the door. A red gleam from inside the building casts a gloomy aura over the darkening day.

'Back then, people with the pox couldn't handle direct sunlight.'

Theodore jumps at the sound of his grandfather's voice, coming from right behind his shoulders. He hadn't heard him approach.

'That's why the windows are tinted red. It also helped for the things they kept in glass beakers. Okay, c'mon, hurry up!'

'Where are we going, Grandpa?'

'We're going to go find her.'

'Who?'

But his grandfather doesn't hear, nor does he wait. He goes slowly down the stairs and keeps walking westward. Theodore follows. They stop for a while in a clearing, where an old foundation with no house left on top of it is fighting a losing battle against the elements. Émeril doesn't say a word. His eyes sweep the land from left to right in an attempt to rekindle his memories, to remember what was here before.

'This is where I was born. The house burned down after we left the island. After the war.'

'Why'd you leave, again?'

Émeril's eyes seem to fog over slightly, but he gets a hold of himself at the last minute. 'C'mon, follow me. We're almost there.'

The two men get back on the road. Émeril speeds up when they walk by another abandoned house.

'This here was the lab. Only certain people were allowed inside. Things happened there. The kind of things you couldn't see, not with your eyes.'

'What about you? Did you go in?'

'Me? I died in there.'

'What?'

Émeril's words hang in the air. He starts walking again; Theodore follows in his footsteps. They pass a narrow building with tiny high windows. A stable of some sort, but its industrial architecture is at odds with the island's other buildings. They keep going. Émeril is finding it harder and harder to walk. His grandson takes him by the arm to steady him. They pass by greyish, poorly maintained houses. Theodore scrupulously avoids looking through their windows out of fear that he'll see a menacing shadow. *This island isn't like other places*, he thinks. It feels as if time has come to a standstill.

'Are you okay, Grandpa?' he asks, looking him in the eye.

Émeril looks suddenly exhausted. His eyes are hollowed out. Theodore feels something balled up in his stomach – a heavy guilt for agreeing to bring the old man here, a fear that he may have put him in danger. Émeril's retirement home has most likely called the police by now. There might even be a missing person report. While Theodore is imagining the worst possible scenario, Émeril stops without warning.

'This is it.'

Theodore looks around. To his right, at the foot of a rocky mount, is a small white church with a red roof. It stands in stark contrast with the rock face, which is darkening as the sun makes its slow descent over the other side of the island. Theodore's grandfather stares glassy-eyed at the chapel. When Theodore touches his shoulder, he startles.

'If you only knew what happened here, on Grosse IÎe, I don't think you'd even talk to me anymore.'

'Well, tell me, Grandpa. I didn't come all this way for nothing.'

'Now's not the time, boy. I don't think I could. But I'm going to give you something. You'll have to take care of it. And then give it to the police. 'Cause of the horseflies.'

'What are you talking about? Why can't you just explain?'

Émeril walks over to the chapel. He follows the white picket fence that marks off the front yard, but instead of going inside he turns right and walks toward the rock face. About two metres up, behind a shrub, there's a limestone hollow built into the rock. A small white cross stands over it. It looks like it once held a small statue.

'There was a statue of the Virgin here. I guess that's why Thomas chose the spot. He must have imagined that no one would lay hands on Mary. That his secret was safe with her.'

'What secret?'

Émeril signals to come over and help him climb up the escarpment. Theodore agrees, and gently supports his grandfather as he pushes him up the rise toward the base of the hollow. Once there, Émeril laboriously kneels down and starts pulling up grass. His grandson helps him. The clay-rich soil is dense, the digging hard. Theodore takes a pointed rock and tries to soften up the earth, while his grandfather sweeps the dirt to one side. Both men are sweating, and Émeril has started wheezing. Finally, around thirty centimetres down, Theodore hits something hard with his rock. His grandfather pulls back his hand and starts scratching at the dirt, carefully now. They unearth a metal box. Émeril pulls it out of the hole. With shaking hands, he cleans it off. It's a touch rusty. He pushes on the lock and the mechanism gives. He breathes in deeply and opens the top. Inside is a small object wrapped in a yellowed pillowcase. Émeril pulls out an old book bound in brown leather. He carefully inspects the pages, testing for water damage. He slides the book back into the pillowcase and puts it in his backpack. An astounded Theodore is about to ask for an explanation when his grandfather puts a finger to his lips. The muffled sound of an engine can be heard.

'Hit the deck!' whispers Émeril, pushing Theodore to the ground.

The two men hide behind a shrub to the right of the hollow while an old jeep drives down the path in front of them. It is probably a couple of Parks Canada employees. The jeep windows are open, pop music pours out. A cloud of dust rises behind it. Theodore's heart races. His mouth is dry, his brain is numb.

Émeril stares at him with the utmost seriousness and then murmurs, 'We don't want them to catch us here. They're touring the island to make sure no one's left. Don't move!'

Theodore doesn't move. He barely breathes. He doesn't think. Seconds turn into minutes. His shoulders hurt, his neck is sore. The engine sounds return, and the jeep drives by again. Then Émeril stands up slowly and starts filling in the hole, carefully replacing the turf. After erasing all trace of their passage, Theodore helps his grandfather down the slope and they walk back the way they came. They are moving much slower now. Theodore's watch shows 7:45 p.m. Only an hour to nightfall. The sun hangs heavy on the horizon.

'Hurry up, boy! Faster!'

They go back along the same route, and it goes much more quickly than on the way in. They stop just a few times, to let Émeril catch his breath. Theodore doesn't take his eyes off the road. In the twilight of dusk, some of the abandoned buildings look particularly sinister. Once they have passed the infirmary and the bridge, they make their way through the cemetery, which gives Theodore goosebumps. Distractedly, he trips on a rock half-hidden by long grass and falls on his side.

'Jesus, watch where you're going!'

Émeril points out the poison ivy next to where Theodore fell. When Theodore gets up, he swears he can make out the same black shadow from before, in the corner of his eye, slipping behind a tree not far from the shore where they first landed. Is it a person? An animal? He looks back in the direction it came from, but sees nothing.

'The dead are all behind us,' Émeril murmurs.

# CAMP DETRICK

*March 9–11, 1943*

They set off early the next morning. Thomas had barely slept. His body was sore from shivering all night, a never-ending series of waves crashing against his bones and skull. Émeril looked no better. His lips were even bluer than the day before. Three non-commissioned officers escorted them to the station. The first train car was reserved for them. Thomas and Émeril weren't allowed to sit together. Thomas stared at Émeril, but his mind was elsewhere. The soldiers made them sit at opposite ends of the compartment and refrain from speaking to each other. The sealed drum of specimens had been loaded onto one of the freight cars. At each station, a different NCO went out to stand guard. Thomas watched them come back in, chilled to the bone, and take turns warming themselves.

The trip took about two days, but as Thomas dozed and slipped between worlds, it felt like a protracted dream. First, they had to get to Montreal, where another train was waiting to take them to Washington. Twenty-nine hours later, when Thomas thought they had reached their destination, the NCOs ordered him and Émeril to get off. Along with the sealed drum of specimens, they boarded a truck and drove north. Two hours later they pulled up at a highly secured facility. Fencing marked off a perimeter so large that no end was in sight. Soldiers were posted at guard stations, machine guns in clear view.

The vehicle came to a halt at the main gate. A huge American flag flew in the air. A few words were exchanged out of Thomas's earshot, and then the gate was raised to let them pass. Ensconced in his seat, Émeril looked tiny. And terrified: even from a distance Thomas could sense his fear, a feeling to which he was not immune.

Several of the buildings were so new that their materials were unblemished, including the two-storey edifice where a dozen soldiers had gathered. Émeril and Thomas were led toward the group. One man came forward to introduce himself: Commander Simon Stevenson, head of Camp Detrick, a research centre for biological and chemical weapons.

The Commander must have been in his fifties. His greying hair did little to camouflage his natural blondness, and he emanated a sense of intractability that Thomas found instantly repellent. The Commander shook everyone's hand and ordered the soldiers to escort the new arrivals inside. Without wasting a moment, petty officers came to collect the drum and lead Émeril away. Thomas stood frozen for a few seconds, and then the Commander gestured to follow them. The small room Thomas was taken to contained only two chairs and a table.

*March 12–April 21, 1943*

The interrogations began. Across from Thomas, a procession of virologists, pathologists, epidemiologists, and some of the United States' best-known entomologists noted down every last detail of Thomas's experiments, discovery, and observations. On several occasions Thomas tried to start a conversation, get some sense of their expert opinions, but each time a soldier called him to order. No matter how many times he asked how Émeril was doing, no one would tell him anything.

*April 22–May 26, 1943*

Minutes turned to hours, hours to days, and days to weeks, and there came a time when Thomas was summoned less frequently for questioning. Most of his time was now spent in a bedroom, where they also brought his meals. He was allowed out once a day to stretch his legs, always tightly guarded. He had no idea whether the specimens they had brought in the drum had been of any use, or if their research had progressed. He couldn't have said whether Émeril had been cured, or even whether his friend was still alive.

Thomas went to bed each night in lower spirits than the one before. His dreams were like gaping black holes, sodden clay soil that clung to his feet and sucked him down toward the depths of the earth. In the images that haunted him, he was fleeing the trenches with Émeril hanging on his shoulders. The ground was strewn with suppurating bodies. Suddenly, they were all coming back to life, trying to bite him with their outsized mouths. A never-before-glimpsed-at horror; a fear spreading through his bones. A scream that reached all the way down into his throat but could never be voiced into notes. Every time he woke he was in the same place. A prisoner. In his cell. In this lab.

*May 27–29, 1943*

Commander Stevenson came to fetch Thomas in person. He and Émeril had been cleared to leave the research centre the following day. He passed Thomas a sealed report and instructed him to hand it over to Major Walker when he got back. On behalf of the U.S. Army and the Allied Forces, he gave Thomas a cursory thanks for his diligence, reminded him of the strict confidentiality of the mission, and wished him good luck in his future endeavours. And that was that. All those weeks without an answer. All those days without knowing whether Émeril had been cured. All those barren hours. Thomas was in shock, his mind AWOL. He could have sworn that his bodily vessel had been ruptured and his soul had departed.

Thomas saw Émeril walking toward him, escorted by three petty officers. He looked to be in better shape than when they'd arrived. His back was a little straighter, and his muscle mass and general vitality seemed improved. But Thomas was struck by something else, a sort of flicker behind his gaze that made him feel like Émeril was going to bite him. Thomas didn't look away, his way of showing his friend that he was with him in spirit. But was Émeril still carrying the virus? Had the anti-rabies vaccines worked? Was he at risk of passing it on to his children? Would the scientists at Camp Detrick pursue their research? Thomas now understood that not one of these questions would be answered.

The return journey was a jumble of confused images and feelings in Thomas's mind. Anger, incomprehension, the signal to leave, a truck, a train; Émeril completely numb, his arms still blue from constant blood tests; soldiers enforcing silence, the train, again, the truck; the military camp at Pointe-aux-Oies, the road toward the shoreline, walking through the green rushes, the familiar, dreadful smell of that clay soil, the St. Lawrence bleeding into the sky, the vertigo of returning to the island, the feeling of suffocating; Émeril's brothers like an apparition, their shadowy bodies, distrusting. Their muscular arms holding their brother; the boat, more of a barge this time, the sound of feet sinking into silt, the suction pulling them down, the regular movements of oars on the water, the pitch and the yaw, the feeling of being the only ones out on the river; and, finally, arrival, relief and fear all together and at once, outstretched hands snatching the report, the Major's gaze as hostile as ever; Émeril's father, hands balled into fists; the soldiers and the other scientists, the dread, the heightened nerves, the foggy brain, Rachelle, his mother, his mother, his own mother, his helpless body in the bed, an anvil, the guilt in every cell of his body, a layer of fatigue coating his bones, his veins, his organs, his muscles, under his skin, lost in the unnameable fog; back where it began, back at Grosse Île.

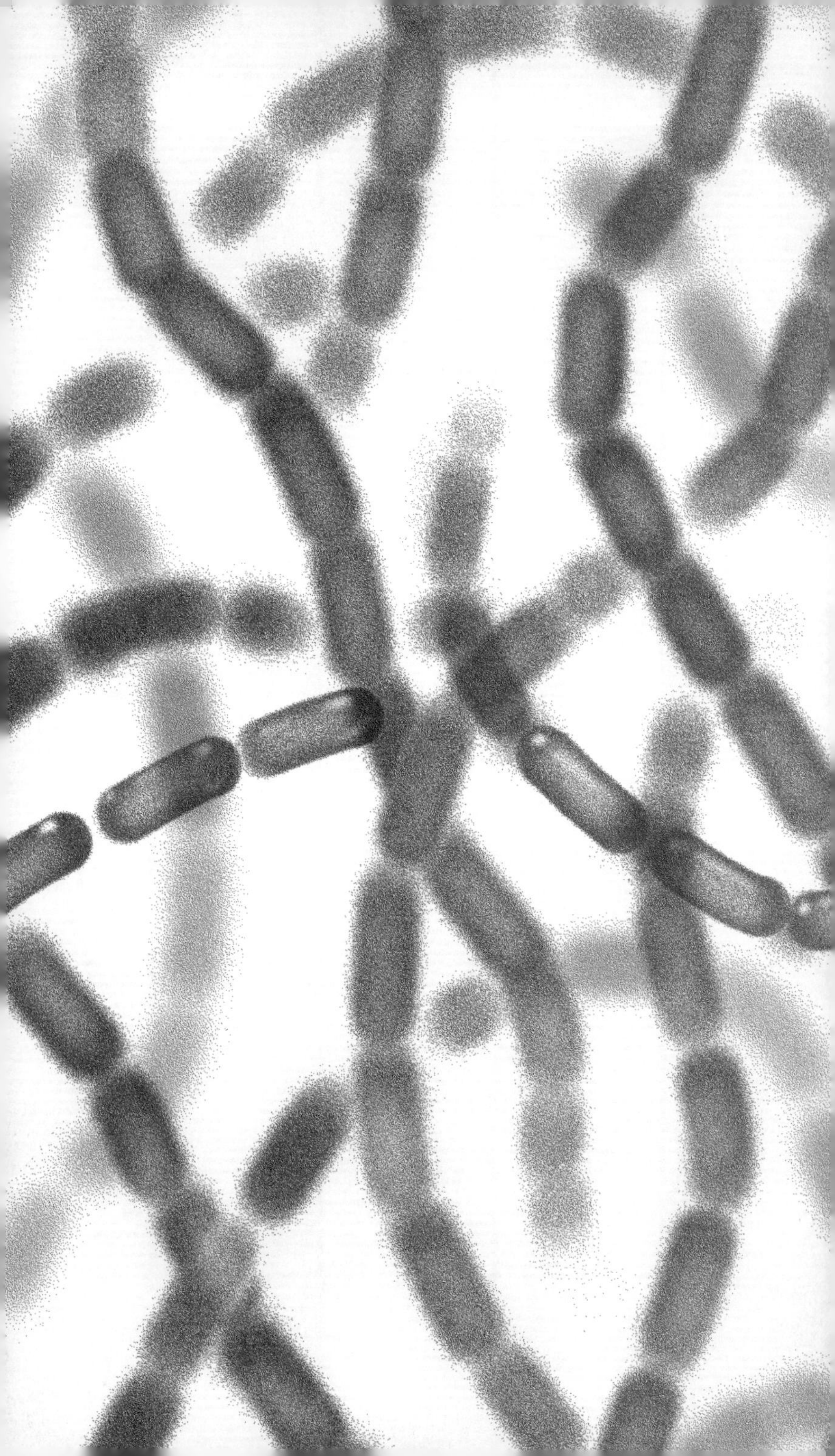

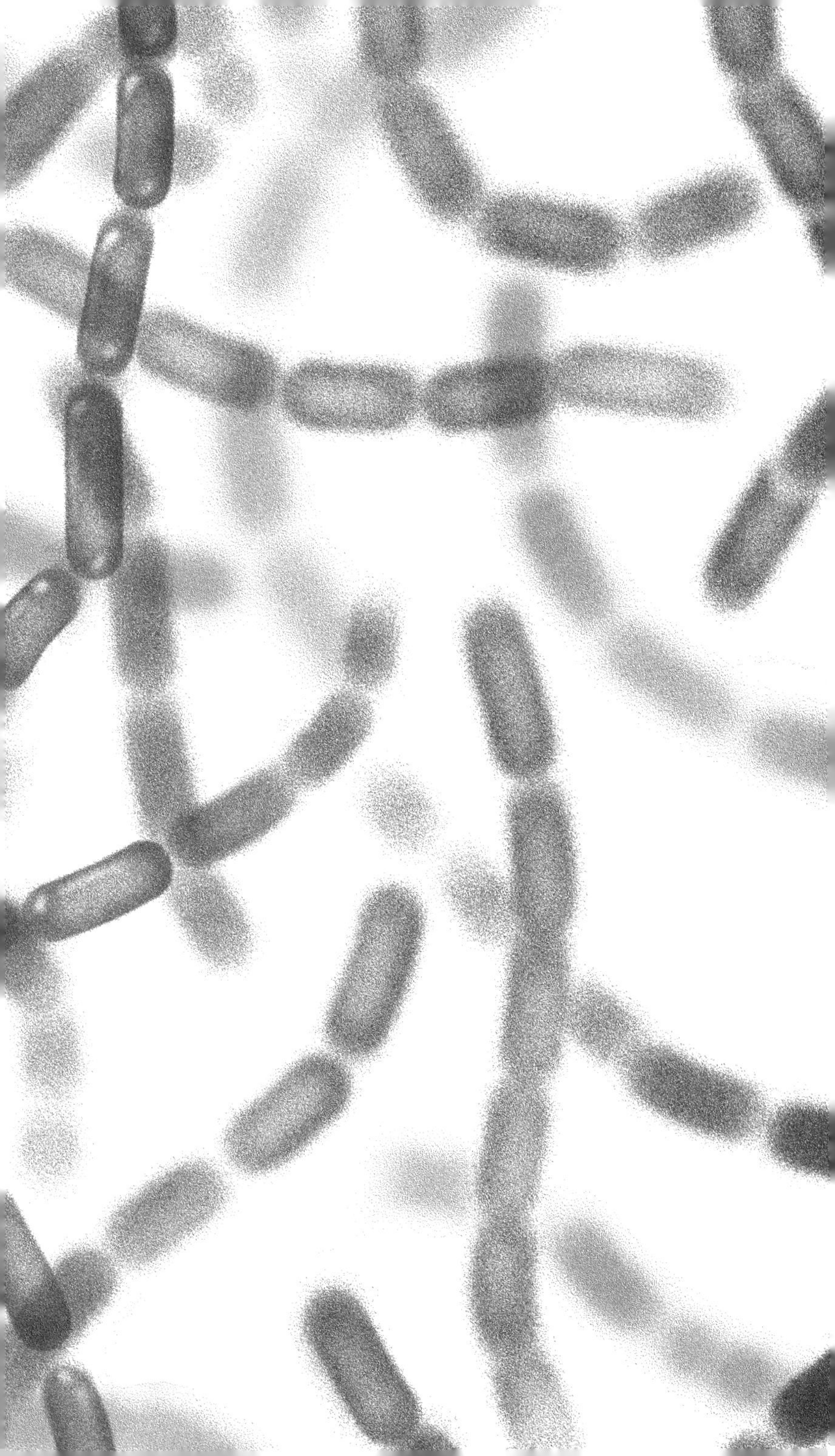

## TRANSMISSION

Time was short, I could tell that my seconds were numbered. I fled your apartment through the tear in the bedroom screen. I left you to your fate, trying with all my strength to suppress the images of our conjoined bodies. My senses were unsettled by the perfect blend of sorrow and rage. I wandered the city for hours, dumbfounded. Only in the morning did I find the north, drawn by the soothing smell of clay. We horseflies do not have noses, strictly speaking, but we can sense smell with our bodies nonetheless. That was how I found my way back to my birthplace on the banks of the St. Lawrence. Nothing had changed: the wet tidal flats, the regular lapping of waves, red sand, polished stone, and a throbbing cloud of insects. Thousands of us shared those banks and our reproductive desires.

While the rising sun cast its rays on the opaque water, I alighted on the tallest of the green rushes. Instinctively my body released pheromones. The males sensed my presence and began flitting around. After thirty minutes of this languorous dance, I flew off to find my chosen one. The males followed me over a hundred metres. I carefully assessed their flying proficiency, speed, acceleration, deceleration, and above all endurance. It took me two hours to winnow down the field to one, the finest of his species. I set my feet down on the culm of a rush, there to wait; sometimes we must abandon ourselves to domination. I let myself be straddled, overwhelmed by my partner's pleasure signals. You may not know that the sexual congress of flies and ejaculation in particular is a gratifying experience for males. I cannot say that I felt the same orgasmic release, but the act of fulfilling my destiny awakened a miraculous excitement in me: a harmony with the future, a paroxysm of pleasure that brought about the sublimation of my selfhood.

Basking alone in post-copulatory plenitude, I slowly digested your blood and your flesh, impatiently waiting for my ova to mature. Four days later I laid one hundred eggs in clusters on a rush. And then I flew off, toward the river this time. I had to get to know my ancestors' birthplace. The island where you first unleashed our fury. I did not turn around to take one final look at my offspring, the larvae that would hatch in five or so days. I was confident that the heat wave was here to stay. You have upset the climate in a way that will perpetuate the cycle. I left their destiny in nature's hands, knowing deep down that my mission was fulfilled. I had passed on to you much more than a mere bite. Our rage would now be yours to share.

## THE FULLNESS OF WATER

The tide is almost high. The water rises up over the last few metres of sand on the mud flats. A heavy silence reigns along the shore. Theodore is relieved to notice that the horseflies appear to have forgotten him. He stares out at the boat bobbing in the distance.

'How will we get back to our boat, Grandpa?'

Without a word, Émeril takes off first his shoes and then his socks, which he carefully folds and places inside them. As Theodore stares in bewilderment, his grandfather removes his belt, undoes the button at his waist, lowers his zipper, and lets his pants drop to the sand. Next he unbuttons his shirt, which he places on top of his pile of clothing. His white undershirt stays on. Again, Theodore notices how spindly Émeril's arms and legs have become. His underwear is riddled with holes, dotted with stains. The liver spots on his skin are a reminder that the path ahead for him is much shorter than the road already travelled. And suddenly Theodore is stung by a thought, painful as a bite: this may be the last moment they share.

Émeril leaves behind his clothes and walks into the river. The water's temperature does not deter him. He calmly advances, while a flabbergasted Theodore stays behind on shore. The sun has reached that point on the horizon where it seems to speed its course before disappearing behind the mountains. Oranges, reds, pinks, and purples bleed together as if someone has blown on the sky with a straw. As he takes in the spectacle, Theodore sinks into his memories. Each and every evening spent helping his grandfather on the farm, chores that were nothing but hateful to him at the time, have become treasured memories. He observes Émeril's steady progress further out and deeper into the water, which comes up to his thighs now. As he is finally getting ready to join his grandfather in the river, a noise from behind startles Theodore. He whips around and sees a moose, standing just a few paces away. The great beast is looking him square in the eye. It has appeared out of nowhere. Its gaze is deep, dark, furious. Theodore can't look away. The animal snorts loudly. Its hooves stomp the ground. Its head swings back and forth. The fur bristles around its neck and back. Its bellow makes it clear that Theodore should leave, but he just can't do it. He's paralyzed. Man and animal stand their ground, staring each other down. Theodore's reflection in its eyes is insignificant, minute, the tiniest of specks. He feels as though it is speaking to him, though he cannot hear a thing. He feels the full force of the animal's rage – a silent, terrible, cold, animate, and legitimate grievance against him and his kind; a volcano ready to erupt; a stream of lava that will flow unchecked over anything that stands in its way, destroying all trace of its passage. The message is clear: a balance lost must be found again.

The moose now flaps its ears, a final warning, and charges Theodore, who throws himself to the ground to avoid it. When he falls he hits his head on a large rock. Though dizzy from the impact, he still manages to spring up onto both feet, fearing the moose will attack again, but it has mysteriously disappeared. Theodore confusedly pans the horizon, a full 180 degrees, but by the time his gaze reaches the river, all trace of his grandfather has vanished.

'Émeril!'

Theodore yells out as loudly as he can; the only answer is a resounding silence. He stares out at the open river. Beyond their boat, a black point emerges briefly from the water and then disappears, carried off by the waves. His grandfather. *His grandfather!* Without taking time to get undressed, Theodore flounders out into the river. A few metres in, there is a drop-off. Theodore is in over his head. He starts to swim, with great difficulty. Despite his determination, he can't maintain his pace. Cold rising currents run through the water, pulling and pushing him to and fro, setting him off course. Unseen hands are holding him back. His grandfather is even further out now. Theodore tries to swim over to the boat, but it too is drifting away from him. His energy is waning. He sees Émeril one last time off in the distance, before the river swallows him. Panic sets in. Theodore is short of breath, his mind in a fog. He starts to sink; he chokes on the water, gasps for air. His limbs feel weighted down. He fights to stay afloat but starts to sink again. Deeper and deeper, Theodore is sinking. Into the depths. The abyss. A heaviness comes over him. Darkness. His limbs. His head. He stops. Darkness. Stops fighting. Spreads out his limbs. Darkness. He lets the water take him. Into its arms. Darkness. Nestled up against him. Darkness. A plenitude seizes his entire self, from every angle. Darkness. The river unburdening itself. Striped bass, sturgeon, eels. The crossing. Darkness. Shore to shore. Past and future. All together. Darkness. Absolute plenitude. Heaviness. The letting go, the leaving of self. To be tossed, to be turned. Darkness. Infinitesimal. Movement. Comforting. To let yourself be pulled back. Oh so gently. The surface. The banks. Silence. Darkness.

When he opens his eyes he believes he is dead. He is sprawled out on the sand, in the bay. How did he get there? The first glints of dawn are furrowing the sky. He tries to find his pulse, locates a rapid and faraway thumping in his wrist. His body is heavy, bulky. He feels feverish. A sour taste clings to his mouth. His normally abundant saliva is scarce. He doesn't know what to do. His limbs are unusually stiff, his neck won't turn. With every ounce of strength he can muster, he pulls himself up on his elbows. Flashes of the night before come back to him. He looks around. No trace of the moose. No trace of his grandfather. Theodore wonders if it wasn't all a dream. He sees the pile of clothing left behind, but Émeril is still nowhere to be seen. The boat is bobbing in the distance. The waters have calmed. The tide swells to its full amplitude. He stands up and starts to look around the bay, hoping by some miracle to find his grandfather alive. His search turns up nothing. Devastated, Theodore collapses next to the pile of clothes. Images of Émeril swallowed up by the water torment him. Tears well up. A crow flies overhead. Its caws echo out over the rocks, and in Theodore's head. The crow traces a series of circles in the sky. Its cawing gets under his skin, right down to the bone. Theodore takes out his frustration by hurling a stone at the bird, hoping to be left alone, but it keeps circling back in a narrowing gyre. Thinking the bird is drawn to his sandwich, Theodore places the bag between his legs and opens it. The old leather-bound book is still there, wrapped in the pillowcase. Theodore takes it out and gently flips through it. Old-fashioned penmanship. A journal. *1942*. Much of what is written here he can't make out. He sits there deep in thought for a few minutes, harassed by the squawks of the crow. When he can't take it anymore he puts the book back in his backpack, throws the sandwich over his shoulder, shakes the sand from his clothing, and walks off toward the river. He puts in first one foot and then the other; legs, thighs, hips, waist. He takes the backpack off his shoulders and holds it above his head, to keep it out of the water. With his left arm up in the air, Theodore struggles to swim out toward the boat, even if, this time, the currents don't faze him. The river is swelling to its apex. He flings the bag onto the boat seat and carefully pulls himself up, taking care not to capsize. Once on board, he looks back and sees the crow standing on the shore, exactly where his grandfather had sat next to the pile of clothing. The bird just stands there, staring at him. Theodore looks away.

He lifts anchor, starts the motor, and sets off for the mainland. He takes several turns around the bay and the neighbouring islands in the hope of finding his grandfather's body, although he knows deep down that this river will never cough it up. Émeril is home. Grosse Île vanishes in the distance. Theodore knows he must act quickly now, hand over the notebook to the authorities. He can feel something changed inside himself. An imperceptible quivering pulses through his bones, through his veins, his organs and muscles, under his skin. Unbeknownst to Theodore, the rage is taking hold of him. While he tries to steer toward Berthier-sur-Mer, he thinks of Marguerite. He wonders if she's safe.

# THE DISMANTLING

*May 31–June 3, 1943*

The Grosse Île War Disease Control Centre was to close, an irrevocable decision set out in the report. Some soldiers blamed the sightings of German submarines out in the river; others believed it was a matter of safety, given the high risk of a leak that had been present from the start. Thomas knew the truth but would not breathe a word of it.

Within seconds, chaos gripped the island. For the soldiers, this meant working even harder to prepare their imminent departure. The cattle and other animals were to be slaughtered and buried on the island. The stable, shed, and lab had to be cleaned out until no trace of their presence remained. A bonfire roared near the bay, and they threw in everything they could. A thick corridor of smoke rose up to the sky, and the nearby buildings were not spared. Under Major Walker's orders, most of the scientists were confined to the hotel, out of the way of the cleanup operation. A steamboat requisitioned in Quebec City to ferry them across the river was slow to arrive. An hour passed, and then two, and then three, and then a day, and then two, and then three. The scientists waited in strictly enforced isolation.

Since getting back from the United States, Thomas had locked himself away in his room. He was unable to get up, incapable even of packing his suitcase. Again and again in a never-ending loop he read through his notebook, unable to stop. He pored over the notes he had made since the discovery. Perhaps he hoped that this rereading might somehow make what was written less true? He was well aware that, sooner or later, he would have to hand the notebook over to the soldiers, who would burn it with everything else. He also knew he would be searched before leaving the island. Still, he could not let the notebook go. Everything he had done and all he was yet to do were slipping away from him. Nothing was left of their island routine save the dining hall bell, which still rang through the hotel at regular intervals, a hollow reminder. As the scientists waited to leave, Rachelle kept on serving their meals. Thomas had made discreet inquiries after Émeril. Rachelle was cold at first, but softened over time; Thomas had always been her favourite. He learned a few things: Émeril was getting better, as far as could be expected. He was hard at work with his brothers and the soldiers, emptying out the facilities. With downcast eyes, Rachelle also admitted that she was looking forward to resuming normal life. Thomas understood; he too longed to leave this cursed island. But his thoughts kept circling back to Émeril. What would happen to him?

*June 4–5, 1943*

08:15. Thomas had gone upstairs after his breakfast. As high tide was reached, he saw through the curtains a steamboat clearing the horizon. Its plume of grey smoke seemed to connect it to the sky. From a distance, the boat appeared to levitate. In the room next to his, a scientist had started whistling. Thomas felt his spirits rising for an instant, just an instant, before a non-commissioned officer burst into his room to crush his stillborn hope.

'Major Walker wants to see you in the laboratory. *Now!*'

Thomas closed his eyes to gather his thoughts. This was the moment he'd been dreading. The previous few minutes had almost convinced him otherwise. He had allowed himself to dream of his old life, to imagine going back to university, seeing his loved ones again, seeing his mother. He had even entertained a fleeting thought that once he got back home he might meet a girl, start a family. It was just one more of his dreams promptly quashed by Major Walker.

Thomas's first instinct was to disobey the order, but the soldier slowly moved his hand to the butt of his rifle. Thomas took a deep breath and stood up. As he walked past the dining hall, he noticed that some of the scientists had gathered near the door. The steamboat had reached the shore; an air of expectation filled the room. The NCO spurred him to move faster. Thomas kept going.

He had taken this route a thousand times before, could have done it with his eyes closed. Down the slope toward the bay, the guard hut, the old cemetery, the back road, the two chapels. The escorting soldier followed a few steps behind. When he got to the lab, Thomas quickly climbed the stairs without waiting for his guard, and went inside. As his eyes grew accustomed to the semi-darkness, Thomas recognized Major Walker, the American anthrax specialist, two other soldiers, and Project F's head virologist. The NCO who had fetched Thomas joined the group. Major Walker was in no hurry. He looked around the group, from person to person, before he spoke. His forehead was sweaty; he did not wipe it. Beads of perspiration slid along his forehead and found a path to his neck, where they slid under his collar. The report from

Washington was tucked under his armpit, dog-eared from being read a thousand times. He closed his eyes, and then, in a single breath, restated the orders he had been given, as if someone else were speaking in his place. No one added a single word, all silently giving their assent. Everyone now understood what was to be done.

08:45. The American, the two soldiers, and Major Walker hurried off to the hangar to start cleaning out the facilities. They emptied out the anthrax spores from the autoclaves and poured everything into drums, which were then hermetically sealed. The orders from Washington were exacting: not one spore was to be left behind on the island. While this was being done, Thomas was to work with the NCO and one of his colleagues to erase all traces of Project F.

The three men put on protective gear. Thomas's first order of business was to tackle the horseflies. Armed with a torch, he methodically burned the insides of each vivarium, making sure that not one single biting fly survived. The wings burst into flames immediately, and the bodies were reduced to tiny mounds of ash that disintegrated into a fine grey powder. Once this operation was complete, the NCO would pick up the cages and burn them in the large fire next to the bay. It was imperative that not one single egg survive. With his torch, Thomas made thorough work of it. The dried insects and those conserved in formaldehyde met the same fate, thrown onto the flames.

The virologist's role was to disinfect the laboratory and equipment with carbolic acid. Every viral sample had already been incinerated. All that remained were the cages, with a few animal corpses inside. They had just received lethal injections. Thomas took off his mask and went off in search of Émeril, who was working with his brothers near the stable. They were shovelling a layer of earth over the last remaining cattle in the mass grave. Émeril didn't seem surprised to see Thomas appear behind him; he had heard the rustling of his protective suit. His brothers glared in distrust, but Émeril gave them a discreet signal to keep calm. Rachelle had been right; he was almost his old self again. His hands had stopped shaking and his face appeared to be at rest. There was a lingering stiffness in his back, as if his bones had been stunted, but still Thomas would never have guessed that he had been contaminated. Émeril was impatient when Thomas asked him to help, but he did it all the same. After going to look for a wheelbarrow, he rushed off toward the laboratory with Thomas. It was the first time they had found themselves alone since their mission to Camp Detrick. Thomas tried to break through, learn a little more about what had happened there, but Émeril wouldn't budge.

'It's not right, what's going on here. You're tempting the devil. I don't want anything to do with any of it. No more,' said Émeril, before his mouth shut for good.

Thomas was quiet. He knew Émeril was right. They started walking toward the laboratory, where the virologist and the NCO were waiting for them to clear out the animal cages. The soldiers couldn't wait to be sprung from this posting. Another ship had been announced to pick them up the next day at high tide. Thomas and Émeril piled the bodies of the animals in wheelbarrows and carried them to the pit, where Émeril's brothers were still hard at work, tossing stiff corpses into the mass grave and covering them with big shovelfuls of earth. Thomas hurried to cover the faces of the monkeys first, unable to face their morose countenances, which seemed to judge them from the beyond. While they finished tamping down the earth on the south side of the stable, Major Walker waved his arms wildly, calling them over to the front of the hangar. Thomas turned his eyes toward them but could not tear his gaze away from the dock, which stood empty behind him. The boat had been gone for hours, taking with it most of the scientists and many of the soldiers. The island was now essentially a ghost town.

12:15. Acceding to repeated orders from the Major, Émeril, his brothers, and Thomas walked up the hill. As they passed in front of the hotel, they glimpsed Rachelle through an open window, cleaning rooms. Thomas waved; she didn't react. Four soldiers in white coveralls came out from the hangar's garage door, rolling drums down to the river, where a canoe had been pulled up. Thomas was horrified to count four in total. They must have contained enough anthrax to kill thousands, even millions, of people. Émeril stared intently at Thomas, as if the results of these calculations could be read on his face. Major Walker ordered them to sink the barrels to the bottom of the river. Thomas had to translate the order. He could barely get the words out of his mouth; each one seemed lost somewhere inside him. Émeril had him repeat the order twice, and then asked what was really in the drums. Thomas was bogged down in silence, unable to answer.

Impatient, the Major signalled to the ice canoeists to carry out his orders. Two soldiers carefully placed the first barrel in the centre of a canoe and weighted down the load on either side. Next, the canoeists and the anthrax specialist gently pushed the canoe toward the water and let it drift a few metres out before taking their seats. Thomas watched them move further out toward the Île la Sottise, tormented by guilt without end.

He had no way of knowing whether the river would one day release these barrels back into the world.

12:45. Major Walker left time for the canoe to make its way around the island and disappear from view, and gave one final order. *Burn the corpse flowers in the marsh. All of them.* Thomas did not immediately react, as he took a moment to assess how risky that might be. By his estimate, the horseflies should be hatching soon. The first ones usually appeared in early June. Could they be eradicated just by burning the plants? Thomas had serious doubts. The Major responded to Thomas's ambivalence by raising his voice. Followed by two soldiers, Thomas started walking toward the marsh. The Major stayed close to the hangar to supervise the loading of the three other drums.

After a stop at the stable to pick up torches and put on protective gear, the three men cut through the forest. Fifteen minutes later they reached the marsh. Thomas signalled to put on their masks and gloves. He did the same. First, the soldiers mowed the tall grass around the corpse flowers to keep the fire from spreading out of control. Then they torched the plants, one at a time, working outward from the centre of the flower, which imploded almost right away. A pestilential odour infested the air. Even with their masks on, the soldiers were nauseated. Thomas's job was to sever the roots twenty centimetres below ground, in the hope that the plants wouldn't grow back next spring.

They worked their way to the middle of the patch. Thomas never knew who saw the first *Tabanus flos cadaver*. He noticed something moving in the corner of his eye. A black speck. He wheeled around. A horsefly had just flown out from the centre of a corpse flower. He stopped in his tracks. Then there was a second one, followed by a third, and a fourth, and then they were coming ten by ten, an army emerging to attack. The soldiers next to Thomas battled on, unaware that they should instead be running for their lives. At the top of his lungs, Thomas screamed at them to torch the flies. The two men did what they were told. Thomas ran over to grab a torch as well, and all three began torching the empty space surrounding them. From a distance they looked like they were fighting the devil with fire. After a few long minutes, every horsefly seemed to have disappeared. Had all the flies been killed? Thomas couldn't say. The three men looked at each other, terrified and wordless. There was not a lot of time. They kept on burning plants and chopping roots with the sole aim of pushing through to the end of this horrible job and getting off the island as quickly as possible. Thomas thought of Émeril. He'd been right. There were roads men should not go down.

18:38. Major Walker came to see them. All the barrels had been sunk. He inspected the work and seemed satisfied. Thomas and the soldiers were famished and exhausted. Not one of them mentioned the incident. They couldn't wait to get back to the hotel. It would be their final night there. As he closed the door to his room, Thomas immediately set about packing his bags. He put away his belongings. When he got to his notebook, he held it in his hands for a long time, lost in thought, and then filled up one last page in diminutive handwriting. He wrapped the notebook in his pillowcase and placed it in the metal box used to store his entomology tools. Then he lay down but did not sleep. Instead, he patiently waited until it was very late, and then got up. He slipped out of the hotel. A full moon lit up the island, casting shadows that swayed eerily. For one final time,

Thomas followed his path to the laboratory, creeping along slowly so no noise betrayed his presence. Purged of its intruders, the island was peaceful at last. Thomas sensed a tranquility, as if the habitual rhythms and breathing of this place had been restored, a dialogue between ground and air. Soon, normal life would resume, for the islanders and for himself.

Just before he reached the lab, Thomas stopped in front of the white chapel. In the moonlight, the church stood out, a starker white against the rock face. A beam of light shone on a small Virgin in the hollow to his right. Thomas walked around a fence and made his way toward her. Mary stood guard over the mount, hands joined in prayer. Her blue eyes seemed to completely absorb Thomas. He got down on his knees and started digging with a rock that he found at his feet. He buried the box with the notebook in it and then slowly set off on the path back to the hotel. Instead of going in right away, he sat on the balcony overlooking the bay and stared east again. Dawn would break soon. For now, the still-dark sky left the stars a few more minutes to shine. Patches of pastel pinks, oranges, and violets appeared, revealing the contours of Île la Sottise, which was gradually bathed in light as the sun approached the horizon. The first rays slapped Thomas hard, with no cloud in the sky to dilute them. Instinctively, he closed his eyes. From head to foot, he was irradiated by something like an electrical current, as if the full power of nature were compressed in a single force now surging through his body. An indescribable heat pulsed through him, a caress like a woman's hand. It was high time to go home.

Thomas sat outside until all the others had woken up and started moving around, making ready to leave. The bell rang one last time, announcing breakfast. Thomas went to say goodbye to Rachelle. She had just received a letter from her husband, was confident the war was coming to an end. Thomas had nothing to reply. When the boat landed, he waved to her one last time and walked away from the hotel without looking back, along with two other scientists, the handful of remaining soldiers, and Major Walker. Thomas was not surprised to see Émeril on the dock. He had known the young man would be there. The two shared a long, intense handshake. Thomas leaned in and, before relinquishing his hand, whispered a few words in Émeril's ear. The men boarded the boat; Émeril tossed out the line. Gently, the boat slipped away from the dock, taking its passengers with it, and the island grew smaller and smaller. In the distance, the houses looked like eyes. Thomas thought he saw an insect.

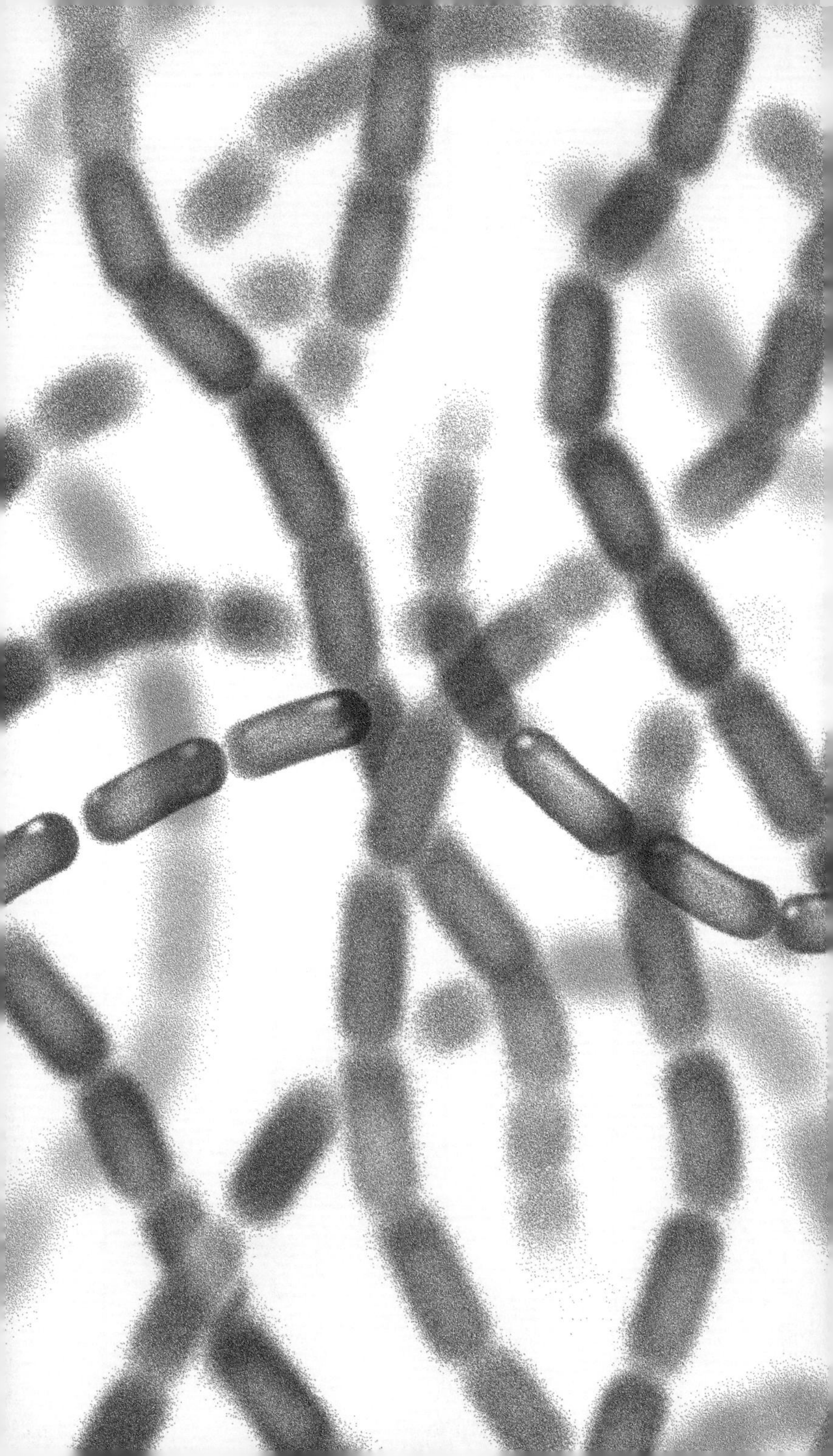

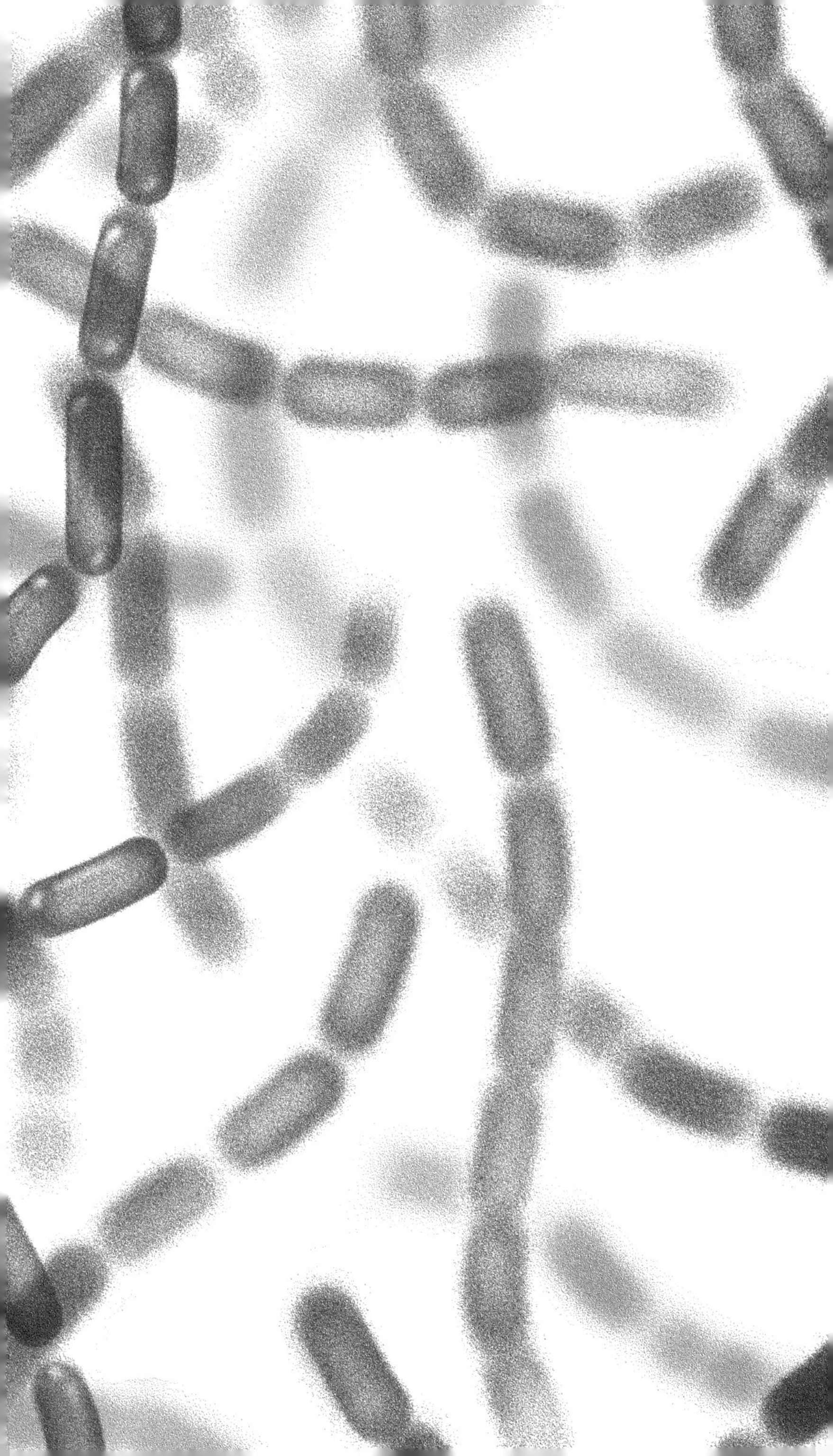

# TOMORROW

I was born in mid-June 2028, along with hundreds of brothers and sisters. We came to life on one of the few islands in the St. Lawrence archipelago inhabited year-round, in the aftermath of an epic storm with winds equal in force and in fury to a hurricane. The air was full of spray, the river's surface covered with patches of drifting foam. Though it was a neap tide, the river was swollen. The wind was blowing in the distance, feeding a swell so strong the river bottom could no longer hold back the waves from crashing full force onto the shore. The current flowing against the rising tides and the unchecked waves so deeply stirred the depths that the buried memories of many years came to the surface.

We hid out in the tall rushes, waiting for this destructive fury to quell. When calm returned, we emerged, shaken but famished, from our hiding spots in the full throes of voraciousness. While you were busy cleaning out your yards and the shorelines ravaged by this unprecedented wave of storms, no one noticed the old metal drum, split open and resting on a sandbar, its spilled contents drying in the sun. We did, though. Nor did you notice us, not at first. You probably felt a visceral fear at the sight of us cresting the banks of the St. Lawrence: a swarm of horseflies, moving as one sombre, voracious mass, caressing the tall grasses at sunrise. You know us all too well. In these last three years, you have tried everything to wipe us out while we have mercilessly infected you, one after another. We have seen you animated by a rabid fury, turning on each other, against your own kind. A deaf, incessant, and destructive anger in which you nearly lose yourselves. You have carried this rage inside yourselves so long; it was no great feat to fan the flame.

I hold out hope that, this time, you will not soon realize what is happening on your riverbanks. That this time you won't manage to stop us. For one thing, on this island in the middle of the river, it will be easy to contaminate each and every one of you. With fierce resolve we will bite you, one and all, and with our hairy feet we will deposit in the wounds that we create those tiny yet terribly dangerous particles whose existence deep underwater you did not suspect. Then, we will set off onto each bank of the river and methodically make our way inland. No matter what happens, our anthrax reserves are more than sufficient for all of you; in addition to the open barrel, the melting permafrost is presenting further possibilities, liberating spores and viruses and bacteria for which you are wholly unprepared. And even if you do manage to stop us, you can count on us to be back. Every tomorrow is a new day.

## NOTE

This novel is a work of fiction inspired by historical facts. Biological research on the cattle plague and anthrax were carried out on Grosse Île, in Canada, between 1942 and 1956. Experimental operations were also conducted by the U.S. Army at Camp Detrick, later Fort Detrick, on the use of insects as potential vectors of transmission. However, the characters and situations depicted in this novel are pure fiction. Any resemblance to real people or situations, past or present, are a matter of coincidence.

## AUTHOR'S ACKNOWLEDGEMENTS

My thanks to Maurice Boissinot, a researcher in infectious diseases at Université Laval, for his passionate and fascinating discussion of anthrax.

I am grateful to Francine Vézina for sharing her experiences of growing up on Grosse Île, and to Laure Guitton-Sert, a post-doctoral researcher in biology, for our far-ranging and surprising discussions.

Thanks to my loyal first readers, Hubert, Louis, Madeleine, Marie, and Judy.

And of course a special thanks to my publisher, Éditions La Peuplade.

## TRANSLATOR'S ACKNOWLEDGEMENTS

Thanks to this book's editor, Alana Wilcox, for her acumen and support, and to the entire Coach House team including James Lindsay, Crystal Sikma, and Stuart Ross.

Thanks also to Aleshia Jensen, first reader of this translation, and to Mary Thaler, for many helpful ideas and suggestions.

I am grateful as well to the author for her assistance throughout the process and for showing me the fascinating history of Grosse Île.

**Mireille Gagné** was born on Isle-aux-Grues and lives in Quebec City. Since 2010, she has published books of poetry, short stories, and the remarkable novel *Le lièvre d'Amérique* (2020), which 'possesses a universal wisdom, the kind that is passed down from generation to generation and from which we too often lose our way.'

**Pablo Strauss**'s recent translations from Quebec include *What I Know About You, The Second Substance, Fauna,* and *The Dishwasher*. He is a three-time finalist for the Governor General's Literary Award for translation. Pablo grew up in Victoria, B.C., and has lived in Quebec City for two decades.

Typeset in Arno, Antique Olive, and Big Cheese.

Printed at the Coach House on bpNichol Lane in Toronto, Ontario, on Zephyr Antique Laid paper, which was manufactured, acid-free, in Saint-Jérôme, Quebec, from second-growth forests. This book was printed with vegetable-based ink on a 1973 Heidelberg KORD offset litho press. Its pages were folded on a Baumfolder, gathered by hand, bound on a Sulby Auto-Minabinda, and trimmed on a Polar single-knife cutter.

Coach House is located in Toronto, which is on the traditional territory of many nations, including the Mississaugas of the Credit, the Anishnabeg, the Chippewa, the Haudenosaunee, and the Wendat peoples, and is now home to many diverse First Nations, Inuit, and Métis peoples. We acknowledge that Toronto is covered by Treaty 13 with the Mississaugas of the Credit. We are grateful to live and work on this land.

Translated by Pablo Strauss
Edited by Alana Wilcox
Cover design by Ingrid Paulson
Interior design by Crystal Sikma
Interior images by Stéphane Poirier

Coach House Books
80 bpNichol Lane
Toronto ON M5S 3J4
Canada

mail@chbooks.com
www.chbooks.com